The Maiden Voyage of
Novyy Mir
And Other Short Stories

Stephen G. Parks

Skrap Books

www.skrapbooks.com

Published by

Skrap Books

an imprint of
Skrap Publishing
Birmingham, UK

www. skrapbooks.com

For everyone taking their first steps

TABLE OF CONTENTS

Last Breath Day

Day 263

Every day is the same: we get up, we work hard, one or two of us die. It hasn't been me yet, obviously, but our numbers are getting down. It'll be my turn soon enough. We call it Last Breath Day.

There were almost three hundred of us in the beginning, the remnants of the Mars colonies. We were given explicit instructions: work to live.

Yesterday was a big assembly day. Whatever they've had us building, it's now in five large pieces — maybe twenty kilometres a side — with perhaps another twelve or fifteen small ones orbiting them. Two of the bigger pieces were finally joined together.

Near the end of our workday, Kayla Wilkins came over and touched helmets with me, which should have given our conversation privacy.

"I can prove it. We're not in Sol anymore. That star," she pointed at the bright yellow-ish disc that was the largest object in our black night, "is Tau Ceti!"

"Kayla, you imbecile, your comm channel's open!" Jed Barkly's voice came through clearly. Leaving the comms open was a foolish mistake and everyone, and I mean everyone, figured she would have her air shortened for that. Jed was just making sure that our overseers would know who to punish for the information spoken.

Kayla's about a decade older than me and was an astronomy

post-doc before the invasion. We all figured she'd be useless at hard labour and would face her last breath day early on, but here she is. Some still say she's useless, but I don't know. They keep letting her live. She must be doing something right.

Of course, they hadn't always been too discrete in who they killed.

Once it became obvious that they were going to kill each of us once they didn't need us, we tried collectively to slow down, to give ourselves a little hope of living longer. Three days in a row, they shorted five of us. By the second day, we were back working at it, full force. They still killed five. And the third day, too. Lesson learned, we didn't try to slow down anymore.

We have an agreement of sorts: on your Last Breath Day, you turn off comms. There's no need to terrify the others, and frankly there's more dignity in being remembered as a hardy co-worker than as a screaming freak begging uselessly for your life.

There were only thirty-eight of us left, the day Kayla misspoke. At dinner that night, no one would sit with her but me. We know they monitor us. The Thurp are often very accurate at who they kill: organizers, rebels, troublemakers…

But somehow, they missed Kayla. The next day, thirty-seven of us came home, including Kayla, but not Paula Glint. She'd died silently working on some task somewhere in our floating hell. Initially, I thought the Thurp had made a mistake and would catch it. Some time later, I noticed that Kayla's air tank had 'Glint' stencilled on it.

Last night she confessed to me that she'd quietly switched air bottles with Paula that day, taking her ration card from her body later. I didn't know what to do, what to say. Should I turn her in? But to who? Besides which, she was letting me sleep with her. I didn't want to lose that.

Day 281

I owe Kayla my life. Two days ago, Kayla helped me finish a bunch of tasks. Each day we get our instructions through a task queueing system in our suit HUDs. You have a task and a duration. Do the task within the duration, get assigned a new task. Fail to do the task … well … learn to breathe very shallowly. I'd gotten behind, couldn't get two pieces to fit, was sure I was going to die.

Barkly was cackling at me. He was shift boss and could see all the reds I was loading up.

"Faster boy," he'd shout into the comms, unnecessarily drawing attention to my failings. "Faster or get ready to die!" He almost sounded gleeful. "Don't forget to turn your comms off, boy! We don't want to hear you squirm."

Kayla had come over and taken on three of my tasks. I finally got the two pieces to align. It wasn't hard once Jed's pressure tactics faded. But I worried that Kayla would pull a last breath day - helping me had hurt her productivity.

Kind of shockingly, yesterday was Jed Barkly's Last Breath Day. He didn't turn his comms off, the bastard. His last words had been, "Kayla, damn you!"

That night, Kayla told me that Jed had been secretly nursing a dislocated shoulder. It had stopped him from being able to complete an assigned task. Kayla had had to crawl into that hole, brace herself and tighten down that joint. She had claimed the completion. Jed had failed to do his task.

Day 285

It's a hard life, with few distractions. We try all kinds of little subversions, ways of secretly rebelling against them. Painting our helmets is just one. Kayla helped me decorate mine, a fancy dragon head design on both sides. She has a simple design, just one stripe. No, she's added another one: two stripes on her helmet.

I'm sure that we all think we're fighting the good fight, the last remnants of humanity not going quietly into that cold, dark night.

Day 288

I do remember seeing Kayla among the survivors when we were first captured, but we didn't talk or really pay any attention to each other. I was still processing the loss of my family; parents and brothers. She'd apparently been widowed in the attack. It was only later that I ended up with her. Still not sure how that happened.

We've got a unique problem developing, pardon the pun. Kayla's pregnant, probably the last human ever to be so. For the first few weeks, she did everything she could think of to terminate it - asking people to punch her in the stomach, injecting weird concoctions, fasting, doing crazy exercises… Still, she's pregnant. Almost five months now. It's hard to hide. She can barely fit into her spacesuit.

Her productivity must be going way down. She can't bend as well, move as fast, or climb into tight spaces … hell, even her stamina is down.

One thing's for sure, the Thurp aren't going to allow humanity to grow in numbers, not even by one.

Day 293

Today's tasks seem to be about fitting smaller pieces to the new large assembly. We're working in small groups today. My assembly team is just me and Kayla. I'm really not happy. I don't want to have to compensate for her slowness, her immobility, but I don't want to appear to be missing my deadlines, either. Ya gotta earn that air.

What the …? I'm getting a red light? Air is critically low and falling fast? That can't be right. Oh, God! It's me … it's me … I'm the one they're shorting? No! It can't be … I've got a full task list today.

Maybe it's a micro-puncture? Where? Where?

"Kayla, come here! Is there a tear in my suit?"

What's she doing? She's coming over too slowly, she's distracted. She's adding a third stripe to her helmet! "Hey, stop smiling … this is serious!"

We touch helmets.

"So lover boy, can I take your ration card now, or do I have to come back when you finish squirming?" she says, smiling. What the…? I … I don't understand. "Don't worry, I'll still name the baby after you."

She pushes off. I can't hear her, but I can see she's laughing. She twists away and I can see my name stencilled on her air tank.

"Damn you, Kayla! No, I won't turn off my comms channel, you little …"

How It Really Happened

For most of them, it was the night sky that gave the first clue. They used social media to meet up, to stand together, ooh-ing and aah-ing as a constant stream of shooting stars rained down on Earth for almost four whole days.

But their leaders knew better.

No artificial satellite could survive that bombardment. Blinded, they could do nothing but await the inevitable arrival of the asteroids.

Of the eight we sent, only five hit – one missed completely, and two glanced off the atmosphere. Nevermind, it was sufficient.

The humans had no colonies. They are no longer a threat.

Sylvester Down

Motor Yacht *Sylvester* was a beautiful yacht, luxurious, easily able to cruise the inner planets. She could even fling up a solar spinnaker for show, a bulbous sail that reflected glorious light onto the ship, making it look like a showpiece, a trophy, almost new.

Not that seventy-five years had aged the yacht substantially. The Creena family had money, and even their antique yachts were continually kept up to code, luckily too, because when you need something like the escape pod, it simply has to work.

It had, mostly.

***

"This is *Sylvester*," Charlan's desperate voice called over channel 17, the one that Orbital Patrol were supposed to monitor. "Mayday, Mayday. We are under attack."

She scanned the screens. There wasn't a patrol ship this side of the Moon. The attacker stayed tucked in so close that scans from Earth wouldn't even see it.

Pripong hit the thrusters, belatedly shouting an acceleration warning. Charlan couldn't brace in time, and cracked her shoulder against the life support console.

"More warning next time!" She shouted.

"Sorry hun, looking for a solution to a problem. Burning full thrust straight for Earth. Let's see what their top speed is."

The 'problem' was easily keeping pace with them. It was smaller, more manoeuvrable, and apparently had electro-static weapons. Charlan couldn't tell if her message was getting out through their attempts at jamming.

Charlan turned to Pripong. "Can we vector our thrust into their face?"

"Not our thrust, no, they're too nimble for that." Charlan knew that tone. Pripong had a solution, a crazy one.

"What are you thinking?"

"Our black water tanks are pretty full…"

"What good does that do us?" Drian asked from the engineering console.

"We can't fight. These pirates are better armed. But we can hope to slow them down, get far enough away for comms to work."

"And spraying them with our frozen shit is going to slow them down how?"

"It won't, but the next part will." Pripong smiled. Charlan hated that smile. That smile had wrecked a Lamborghini in the Alps. That smile had put massive dents in the hull of this very yacht more than once.

That smile would get someone killed some day.

***

Any landing you walk away from is a good one, Charlan thought as she rubbed her sore shoulder, even if that landing is in an escape pod.

She popped the hatch. A quick look around confirmed what she'd seen out the portal.

"We landed near the equator." She smiled, trying to find a way through her captain's rising sadness. "No, better, we landed on the beach of a small island near the equator. Damn fine flying, if you ask me."

Still, Pripong didn't nod or smile. He kept looking at the controls, deep in thought, near tears.

"Cap'n?" Drian added, "You did good. You got us down in one piece, alive."

"Yeah, thanks," Pripong's response sounded automatic, disconnected.

"I'm sure Matthew's OK." Charlan lied, adding, "We called the cops. They'll find him."

"Yeah, OK." He wasn't convinced. He wasn't sobbing, but she could hear the tears in his voice. Charlan had a flash of doubt, wondering if he would have been this concerned if it had been her missing.

"In the meantime," she continued as Drian and Sebu pushed past her and tumbled out the portal, "We're at a beach. It's high noon on a sunny day, and Rescue won't be here for a few hours at least, so how about we have some fun?"

Pripong never said 'no' to having fun, until today.

Charlan shook her head, jumped carefully out of the hatch, landing on the moist sand of the receding tide. The occasional wave splashed her feet, cool against the heat of the sun. She walked up to where small shells littering the beach along the high tide mark.

Charlan tried coaxing Pripong out of the capsule. She suggested that they go swimming. She stripped down to her underpants, then realized her mistake. Pripong may not be interested in her bare breasts right then, but Drian and Sebu were staring. A quick reversal and a t-shirt covered that up.

"Hey cuz, you really don't know what you just missed." Sebu shouted into the capsule.

"Pthh," Drian grinned, "He's seen 'em before."

"Oh, grow up," she chided Drian. At least Sebu, Pripong's young cousin, had the excuse of being a teenager. Drian was in his thirties, and married. He should know better than to leer.

***

Deep in the sky overhead, where they'd lived until just recently, the Orbital Patrol were scanning near space for pieces of wreckage, navigational hazards, salvageable pieces, clues to a crime, and perhaps a missing person.

"We found another piece of wreckage from the *Sylvester*. Permission to push it into atmo?" Patrol K4 asked.

"Negative." The radio crackled. "They're reporting one crew member not accounted for. This is a rescue mission until we've exhausted all hope."

"Shit. Look at that piece of wreck, tumbling. It's gonna take twenty percent of our RCS just to bring it under control. Then we have to board?"

"Affirmative. This is designated as an R&R."

"Acknowledged," The patrol officer wondered which R it would be, a rescue or a recovery. Rescues could be fun, especially from these rich super yachts. Grateful survivors often tipped well.

Recoveries, well, recoveries were never fun in zero G. They often involved vacuum cleaners.

***

"Ready?" Pripong asked Drian as they incrementally changed the lateral rotation of the ship, trying to disguise their intent.

"Ready!" Drian shouted.

"Charlan?"

Charlan could see Pripong's problem; Earth was getting bigger on the view screen by the second. To carry out their plan, they had to turn the ship away from a landing approach. Worse, they couldn't decelerate.

"Ready." She said, even if she wasn't convinced.

"Go, one!"

Drian flipped a switch and watched with pride as the Sylvester's blackwater nozzle flooded the attacker's flight path with liquified human feces. Aimed close enough to their own exhaust, it should still be liquid when it impacted the pirates.

He called out the levels, "Tank will be depleted in three …
Two… One."

"Go, two!" Pripong commanded.

Charlan released the solar spinnaker. It wouldn't get to its full
deployment, but the bunched up cloth would definitely hit the
pirate ship and spread around it.

Charlan watched carefully. As soon as she saw signs of impact,
she cut the shrouds. Immediately, their radio was flooded with a
jumble of urgent communications. The mylar of the spinnaker
apparently defeated the electro-jamming.

"Mayday, Mayday. This is *Motor Yacht Sylvester* being chased
to atmo by a pirate! Mayday!" Even as she spoke, the *Sylvester*
slammed down and to port. Pripong's wide-eyed expression
confirmed to her what she needed to say next. "They're firing on
us! Mayday! Mayday!"

Charlan could see Drian's terrified expression. He might be
gruff and tough, but being the recipient of outright violence was
outside his experience.

"Port RCS are all depleted, starboard down to ten percent
and we're venting. We're going in, no way around it." Pripong
looked around desperately. "We have to abandon ship. Where's
Matthew? Where's Sebu?"

Both Charlan and Drian shook their heads. They hadn't had
time to worry about those two.

The ship started to shake, gaining intensity with each bump.
Upper atmosphere was approaching far too quickly. Pripong
picked up a mic. "Abandon ship! Sebu? Find Matthew and meet
us at the escape pod."

***

Lacking leadership from Pripong, Drian started making
decisions on his own; decisions that Charlan wouldn't have agreed
to. Even though she had the most experience on yachts, she was

officially just the captain's girlfriend. Drian was the senior paid crewmember, and he wasn't about to listen to her.

He'd taken a bucket and started scooping sea water into the escape pod.

"It's too hot out here. I want a cool bath!" He laughed as he tossed a second bucket to Sebu, who quickly joined in.

"Don't let the water level get as high as the food stock," Charlan warned, but Drian dismissed her with a "yeah, yeah," and kept going.

Pripong, sitting in the shade of the capsule, was finally talking, shock finding expression, grief looking for solace.

"For seventeen years, that ship's been my life, my home." Charlan pulled him away from the others. His tears started to flow freely. "And we didn't all make it. Matthew didn't make it."

"They'll find him."

"Hey Charlan," Drian shouted to their retreating backs, as he reached down and scooped another bucket of sea water, "why don't you take your shirt off again, see if that helps."

Her reply to Drian was her outstretched middle finger.

***

"This is Orbital Patrol K4." The radio crackled, drawing Pripong and Charlan back into the cockpit even as Drian sprinted for the escape pod. "We're vectoring in. ETA three minutes. What's your status?"

"K4, this is *Sylvester*. We're abandoning ship. Now."

"Understood. We will track and recover. Can you identify your attacker?"

"We can't, but you can. We sprayed the ship with black water. When it hits atmo, the shit will all burn off, giving you a really nice smoke trail to follow. And no matter what port they try to hide in, theirs will be the ship with extensive scorching on their forward hull."

"Uh… OK? Understood *Sylvester*." Charlan could almost hear the pilot thinking, you're a weird one. "Good luck. K4 out."

They arrived at the escape pod at the same moment that Sebu did. Alone.

"Where's Matthew?" Pripong's voice was almost shrill. Charlan grabbed his arm to stop him from running off to look for Matthew. A nod to Drian, and they pulled Pripong into the escape pod.

"Matthew will be OK," Charlan tried to comfort Pripong.

"That's bullshit and you know it."

"Fine, but right now, you need to pilot this damned thing down there." She grabbed his head, made him look into her eyes. "Save us."

With the hatch closed, Drian pulled the lever, sending the pod out into the atmosphere. Automatic stabilizers controlled the descent for the first ten seconds. Pripong seized the moment to grab the shortwave. "K4, this is *Sylvester's* escape pod."

"We are tracking you."

"Four souls onboard. One soul unaccounted for."

"You left…?"

"We couldn't find Matthew!"

Charlan heard the deeply frustrated grunt from the patrolman. "Understood. Disengaging the pirates, commencing search and rescue."

***

Charlan wasn't used to Pripong caring about others. This level of emotional display was unique in her five years with him. The only time she'd ever seen him cry had been on the eve of his thirtieth birthday. That'd been self-pity.

Where was this coming from?

"Are you worried about what your father will say?"

"My father? I'm a grown man. I'm not afraid of my father." Charlan liked Pripong, she really did, but he wasn't a grown man. He was a trust-fund baby, and that always stunted emotional growth.

Pripong sputtered, "I lost *Sylvester!* What will Grandpa say?"

***

"Command, this is K4. We've secured a section with life support." Even with a crew of only three, the patrol craft was spacious for a reason. Prisoners, rescued people, medical emergencies. Cubic space on a patrol craft was available for any contingency.

"Follow full procedures. Bring him back safely."

"Affirmative." K4 extended a large, fragile tube of mylar surrounding a thin scissoring framework. Once it made a seal, the tube pressurized. Two patrolmen went down and checked before starting the cutters. "We have a seal. We're still not getting any comms chatter from inside."

It didn't take long to breach the hull. It took even less time to find Matthew.

"Oh, you're fucking kidding me!"

***

Charlan noticed it as soon as she and Pripong started walking back: the escape pod had tilted further. The beacon lights weren't blinking anymore.

"What happened?" she ran up. Drian's face was a mix of anger and dejection. "You put in too much salt water, didn't you? You fried the electronics! The locator beacon?!"

Her accusation was met with an apologetic shrug. Sebu was biting back laughter.

"Well, we're going to be here for the night now." Charlan pointed to the clouds brewing on the horizon. "And I'm willing to bet that that's a thunderstorm heading our way. But hey, at least we have shelter. Oh, wait, it's full of water. You fucking idiots!"

***

It would have been a nice, refreshing breeze that accompanied the dawn's sun, if they weren't all soaking wet, shivering, and hungry. No fire had been possible in the storm, no food had been salvageable. The escape pod was unusable. Between the strong winds, rain, and the storm surge, the capsule was partially submerged, rocking gently in the surf.

Above them, they heard a sound. A ship was approaching. Sebu was the first to cheer. Orbital Patrol had found them. It slowly buzzed the beach, as they waved ecstatically.

Patrol ship K4 landed a ways down the beach, the ship's ramp lowered to disperse two tired officers.

"Are you the crew of *MY Sylvester?* We've been looking for you all night."

"Yes, thank you!" Charlan led the ragged group toward safety, warmth, and the end of their little adventure. "Thank you for finding us."

"Is this your cat?"

"Matthew! You're alive!" Pripong ran past Charlan, grabbing the dishevelled cat. Matthew didn't seem happy, but he definitely knew his daddy, and started purring.

"Sorry about all this," Charlan tried to sound conciliatory between her chattering teeth. One of the officers handed her an emergency blanket.

"Are you the captain?" He asked as she unfolded the thin, warm blanket. She helpfully directed the officer's attention away from her wet t-shirt, towards Pripong and his purring cat.

"Filing a false report with OP is a criminal offense." The patrolman started reading to Pripong from a pad, as they walked aboard K4. "Abuse of OP resources usually equates to forfeiture of your ship, but that's gone. The owner will be billed for our expenses and a hefty fine will be added."

The patrolman flipped to a new screen. "However, we did find your attackers. They were identified in the port of Shanghai with scorch marks all over the hull and even pieces of your spinnaker still draped on the ship's antennae. There is a substantial reward for their arrest. It will… mitigate… part of… Is he even listening?"

"Hey guys, Matthew's purring!" Tears streamed down Pripong's face. "Purr, Matthew, Puuurrrr!"

Charlan sighed, giving the patrolman's shoulder a conciliatory pat, "For what it's worth, there'll be a substantial tip."

Provenance

The satellite definitely isn't American.

ESA, Russia, and China all deny its provenance too. So the Americans decided to crack this mystery open, see who complains.

Hanson intercepts it slowly. Thrust. Glide. Adjust. Repeat. At three metres, she reports in. "It looks like rock. Are you sure it isn't?"

"It's pulsing in high band UV."

A minute later. "Contact! Feels like rock."

A shiny round orb scurries around the rock, stares at Hanson.

"Um, guys, it's alive!"

The orb blinks. Hanson's suit dies. She drifts off, spinning slowly.

Below, she can see the cities on Earth's night side going dark.

The Maiden Voyage of Novyy Mir

I

The banging on his door brought Jack Cogsworth out of his drunken sleep. Military Police met him when he opened the door; not the usual complement of two, but four of them. Apparently they'd thought he might not be alone, and had sent an escort for the lady, too. Either they hadn't heard about the divorce or they didn't know that just being an astronaut wasn't enough these days to have the ladies lining up to share his bed.

Thirty minutes later, hair still damp from the quickest shower he'd ever taken, Visine still drying in his eyes, Jack walked into a NASA briefing room, and right into the face of Kevin Winchester. They scowled at each other as Winchester stood aside, letting Jack see that he was likely the last to arrive.

Whatever briefing had started the meeting, it had obviously passed. Now the important people were in break-out groups, discussing their jurisdictions, needs, and solutions. The important people didn't include Jack, or Winchester, or any of the other astronauts present.

Jack resented the emptiness of his bed even more. Why disturb him if only to ignore him? He knew that the only reason the astronauts were there was so that publicists could say they were. The astronauts would have nothing to do, no input to give, until the mission was drawn up. But once it was, it'd be too late for input from the astronauts.

Such was the life...

Unattended, Jack wandered around.

On the walls were schematics and plans of the International Space Station, not all of them familiar to Jack. Military intelligence was present in the person of Colonel McMurtry, a face known to every astronaut, even ones whose missions didn't include military components. Astronauts tended to see things they weren't supposed to talk about and needed to know to shut up. McMurtry was the reminder.

But now, it looked like he was the project leader.

Jack sighed. He tried to avoid military-related assignments. His career path hadn't included military service and hated the attitude. McMurtry running the show, whatever this show was, wasn't a good sign.

Nine months earlier, the so-called year-long "Russian tenure" at the International Space Station had commenced, a small price to pay to end a land war in Europe.

But then the station's albedo began to change. The ISS was getting bulkier but, counter-intuitively, darker. Once it became undeniable, it became necessary for the US to have a response.

Jack had a feeling that he knew exactly what this mission would be: Go to the ISS and board it, lay squatters claims to the American side.

He had no desire to get into a zero-G pissing match. Things had a habit of bouncing up there, and bouncing, and bouncing: consequences, most of all.

Standing to one side was a cluster of astronauts, ignoring and being ignored by all. Jack headed toward them. "What are the Russians doing to it?" Jack asked the man beside him, Will Grimes, one of the younger astronauts.

"Best we can guess, they're reinforcing it so that it'll survive a break from orbit." Grimes saw the disbelief and confusion on Jack's face and nodded sympathetically. "I know, crazy."

"Where are they going to send it?" Jack asked.

"They figure the Moon." Grimes didn't sound as if he believed the words he was saying. And by 'they', Grimes meant the brain trust at the front of the room, McMurtry's people.

Jack hadn't liked the idea of the 'Russian Tenure.' In the back of his mind, Jack had always wondered why they wanted it. It seemed so unimaginative. Well, they'd shown him. He hadn't imagined this, they had.

"The Moon? I don't get it."

"You missed the briefing. China's about to launch its first manned expedition to the Moon; India's two years out at best. We've already been there and are about ready to return. Russians have lived with not being first; they can't live with the embarrassment of being third or fourth. They don't have the lift capacity to go to the Moon, but they can load up the ISS and take her."

"So they're going to steal the ISS?" Jack, still a little drunk, spoke his astonishment a little too loudly.

"Be careful with that term." McMurtry looked up from his own personal confab to address Jack directly. "They do own almost half of it. And frankly, we keep talking about defunding our side. Can you steal what's been discarded?"

"There's no way you weren't aware of this," Jack replied to McMurtry, and was met with a bunch of high-ranking heads suddenly swivelling towards him. Oops. He chose his next words carefully, "It's ... become obvious to amateur astronomers. With our gear, we've known for a long while. I'm positive."

"We've watched it develop with great interest." McMurtry conceded dismissively before turning back to his power group; the astronauts once again relegated to back of mind.

A NASA publicist handed Jack a cup of black coffee, and a look of reprimand. Showing up drunk? The look said, Not the right stuff. As if she'd know. He tasted the coffee, almost put it aside. But the other astronauts were all giving him meaningful stares. It was their reputation, too. He drank the wretched concoction deeply.

"You honestly think they can boost the ISS out of orbit without it shaking apart?" Jack asked a rep from Rand, who shrugged. A small group of contractors, as much out of the decision loop as the astronauts, instantly formed around Jack, the lone astronaut brave enough to wander among them.

"We don't think they can do a proper lunar orbit insertion." One defence contractor confided to Jack. "Either they'll crash or they'll overshoot. We've got the most experience on lunar orbital insertions, so we need to bring that with us, use it as a bargaining chip."

"Bring it with us? Bargaining chip?"

"We want a peaceful end to this." Jack startled at the voice behind his ear. McMurtry had walked up behind Jack again. Apparently, Jack was on his radar and it was locked in. "We're bringing in Bryan Clegg. You've worked with him?"

"Yeah," Jack liked Bryan, a good solid flyer, lost to the private sector and a better paycheck. Jack added, "Before he jumped to SpaceX."

"And you know that he flew a Dragon capsule to the moon and back: Did the insertion manually, stayed for six days, came home safely. We've seconded him. He's the most experienced pilot we have for this job."

"OK, am I on the team?"

"Yeah, someone has to be the commander," McMurtry was dismissive, almost seemed to be trying to make a joke. It certainly didn't feel like a resounding endorsement. "Clegg's never manually docked at the ISS. You have, three times."

"Ok…" Jack accepted that. He had docked at the ISS three times, but twice had been assisted 'soft docks.' Only once had he actually done a manual 'hard dock.' Everyone who had been on the station then would remember that docking for the rest of their lives. A little too much thrust and a big, scary noise later, and Jack was no longer a hard dock virgin.

"And who else are you sending?" These new capsules had room for seven and the rockets had lift to spare. In many ways, it was the best time to be an astronaut, especially if the promised big projects - Mars, Europa, Ceres - got their funding.

"Only three of you this time. We're converting the other four slots to supplies."

Jack had a sinking feeling. "Who's the third?"

"Kevin Winchester." Jack turned to find Winchester a few feet away, watching.

"You know my objections to him: untrustworthy, deceitful. He's not a team player."

"But he's competent. No one's ever questioned his competence."

"He single-handedly ruined my marriage." Jack started to thump a finger into McMurtry's chest, then realized who he was addressing.

"He's the right person for the job." McMurty was surpassingly calm in his reaction to Jack's outburst. "He's got military intelligence clearance and experience on the station. He's level-headed, something you could learn. And he knows some of the Russian players, as do you."

"Oh?" Jack just knew what was coming next. There was only one way this could get worse.

"Olga Krenchova is the Russian mission commander." It got worse.

Jack's claim that, "She hates Winchester as much as I do," was met with a dismissive shrug.

II

During briefings, Jack was given access to eyes-only intelligence reports, the type that weren't even allowed to leave the table they were sitting on. The Russians had braced the entire hull of the ISS with a series of girders. The reports noted that even the heat exchangers and solar panels had been extensively reinforced.

They wouldn't attempt tucking them away and reinstating them. Someone had decided that it would be better to strengthen them and ride out the reverberations. Jack shook his head at that. The solar panels were damned flimsy. It really wouldn't take much to break them.

All in all, the new and improved ISS, renamed *Novyy Mir*, looked ugly, like an oil rig wrapped around a submarine. But intelligence claimed it might actually work. The Russians had added modified Angara rockets to the girders. Each rocket could be jettisoned once it had given them more orbital velocity.

The last Soyuz had brought a prototype lunar lander for them to use. Somehow, American intelligence hadn't known that they had a working prototype, never mind a human-rated lander. Jack read that with skepticism. It probably was the untested prototype. Would they have even bothered with the human rating?

Russia was ready to make its move, so NASA had to be ready, too.

Against Jack's repeated objections, 'mission specialist' Kevin Winchester was approved for his crew. Winchester had been on Jack's last mission. It hadn't been a pleasant experience. Jack had gotten along well with the Russians on the station, too well for Winchester's liking. Winchester had done whatever he could to sabotage Jack's working relationship with the crew, especially Olga Krenchova. In the end, they all had parted bitterly.

Jack wasn't sure why Winchester hadn't gotten along better with the Russians. In a lot of ways, Winchester seemed more Russian than the Russians: hard-nosed, with a mean sense of humor mixed with a violently militaristic worldview. He'd have fit the stereotype except for his disdain for alcohol.

Jack couldn't prove anything but he was certain that it was Winchester who had started the rumour about Jack and Olga. There was nothing to the rumour, but its very existence had given Jack's wife the ammunition to file for a divorce.

The mission goals sounded simple but were infinitely complex: Board *Novyy Mir* and take command away from the Russians. What could be easier? What could be harder? Then what? Jack's mission briefing didn't cover that. He wondered if Winchester's did.

Long before NASA could launch, the briefing stated, the Russians would have had time to alter the station's course to create a slingshot effect and send the ISS towards the moon, maybe not at Neil Armstrong speeds, but still at a good clip.

So intercepting the station would have to occur in deep space, between the Earth and Moon.

"Can't you just shut down our side?" Bryan Clegg asked in one briefing. "Make it useless to them? Wouldn't that be enough to keep them from trying this crazy stunt?"

"They've put up signal jammers. We can't talk to our side of the station." Even as McMurtry spoke, Jack noticed a sly smile on Winchester's face. Winchester knew more than Jack did. That had to change.

"But you still have a way to do it. His face," A stabbing finger at Winchester, "tells me so."

"Not quite, but the reclamation systems on our side only work as long as they receive 'go codes' every 24 hours. No go code for three consecutive days and they shut down. Their reclamation system, well, sucks, comparatively."

"I remember. When did the jamming start?"

McMurtry looked at his watch. "Seventeen hours ago."

"So they don't know yet." Jack sighed and shook his head. "They'd be committed to going the whole way to the Moon, then their newly commandeered vessel would start shutting down on them. Let them go or stop them. Don't cripple them halfway. That's a death sentence."

But then, he realised, that's the stick. Put them in a bad spot so they have to accept the carrot - the American mission could restart the reclamation systems and whatever else had security lockdowns triggered.

III

McMurty's boarding procedures and scenarios included ones where they were greeted warmly and ones where they weren't.

"You want us to take guns?" Jack asked incredulously.

"One gun," a nod towards Winchester, the mission's designated muscle. "Rubber bullets."

"And that's safe enough? Strong enough to be useful, weak enough not to puncture the station?"

"It would take... an unfortunate shot... to puncture the hull," McMurty said. Jack scowled at Winchester. *I bet you're trained on how to take those unfortunate shots.*

"I have a question sir," Bryan Clegg actually put his hand up. Jack smiled. *The guy's been to the Moon and back and he still raises his hand in briefings!* "While we're up there, what are you going to be doing down here, sir?" Clegg asked.

"What do you mean, son?" McMurtry stopped the briefing animation and looked at the youngest of the three astronauts.

"Well, what they're doing is an act of piracy. But once they declare it a Russian ship, what we're planning to do will be an act of war." Clegg was mid-thirties, with an expecting wife - their third, if Jack remembered right. *No man wants to raise his children in a world at war.*

"Don't you worry about that, son. You'll come home a hero." McMurtry seemed to think that was an answer, but Clegg didn't.

"I'd rather come home to a peaceful world." Clegg almost sounded like he was talking down to McMurtry. Jack watched with interest. He hadn't seen this side of Clegg before. Maybe private industry had been good to him.

McMurtry didn't bother to hide his frustration at the response. "That's what we're working for."

"But sir," Clegg kept pressing, "if that were the case, then why not just let it go?"

"Can't let them do that, son." McMurtry's anger was starting to bubble up. "Gotta show them that we're in charge."

Clegg shifted his gaze to Jack, as if to ask if he believe this hawkish line of reasoning. Jack just shook his head, looked down, and mumbled, "Sure sounds peaceful to me."

IV

Jack and his crew sat in a private viewing room at the Kennedy Space Centre, watching the data as the ISS's elliptical orbit began to pick up speed with each circuit. He figured three more orbits, and they'd have escape velocity. Just as long as their aim was good. He stared at the data point projected over the world map, willing it to be correct.

Godspeed you crazy Russians! In his mind, he toasted them with an imaginary shot of vodka, to Olga and her three companions.

****

The next day, at T plus forty-seven hours, the crew's simulator training was interrupted when a voice suddenly called out on their headsets, "The Chinese have launched."

"Seriously? They're going for the moon?" Heads everywhere bounced up, tasks forgotten. Jack climbed out of the simulator first and squeezed through the suddenly crowded corridors leading to the control room.

"Launch profile fits lunar." Telemetric data started appearing on one of the world overlays showing a launch from the Gobi desert, the Dongfeng Spaceport for sure. "But they're going fast."

"And three months early. Gotta beat the Russians." People within earshot shook their heads. There were always delays, unexpected complications. Everyone in the room was thinking, you rarely launched on time, never mind early. What shortcuts must have been taken, what risks accepted?

"What're the odds that they'll succeed?" Jack asked the room.

"Realistically?" The designated point-man from Rand spoke as if to say, 'you have to ask?' "Not good. They were rushing their program to begin with. Didn't want the Russians to beat them. Gossip from their taikonauts is that they're all afraid their lander is a death trap. Intel says their orders are to go down, anyway. Come back or stay down, but put Chinese footprints on the Moon before the Russians arrive."

"This is just one big pissing match." Bryan Clegg shook his head.

"You're all too young to remember," McMurtry spoke as he entered the room, "but it was in the old days, too. Back then, we won, so we don't feel the same need to prove ourselves this time. Not for the Moon anyway. If they were shooting for Mars, it'd be a different story."

McMurtry looked over his three astronauts carefully. He handed Jack a folder marked Launch Authorization. "Your launch has been moved up, too. You go tomorrow."

Jack couldn't help but wonder what shortcuts his side had just authorised.

V

T minus thirty-seven hours, thirty-four minutes
Jack decoded and read a scrambled message carefully twice before sharing the details with his crew. "The Chinese missed the Moon. They didn't complete an orbital insertion. They slingshotted around instead."

"Shit. How many people?" Clegg wanted to know how many had just been sentenced to death. Jack didn't have any answers.

He hadn't followed the details of the Chinese mission at all. His focus had only been on his own problems. What would happen when Novyy Mir was confronted by the gun nut sitting beside him?

Over the course of the next few hours, the news got a bit more hopeful and detailed. The Chinese may have managed a complete slingshot and might be Earthbound. NASA couldn't confirm that yet, but there was that little bit of hope for the now-confirmed three taikonauts.

T minus forty-three hours and seven minutes
Ground control sent up an urgent message. 'Large reflective object has separated from ISS. Possible catastrophic structural failure. Beware of debris.'

Jack looked at Clegg, their pilot, who said, "It's not like we can swerve to avoid it."

"No, or even slow down," Jack agreed. None of them had signed up for a demolition derby in space. "But keep your helmets nearby. Gloves too. Sleep fully geared and strapped tight. Be ready for decompression."

"We didn't have this on my last trip out," Clegg tried to joke, but it fell flat.

"Winchester, can you get on the scrambler and ask some of your intelligence buddies if they know what the hell's going on over there?" Winchester nodded. He was worried too.

It took a few hours, but he got to the right people, eventually. "It was their lunar lander. They jettisoned it. We think." Winchester still had a hand on his earpiece, looking off occasionally as some voice or another talked to him.

"We think? How sure?" Even as Jack asked, he saw Clegg mouth 'We?'

"Positive it was their lunar lander — that we know — but it may have changed course after leaving."

"Manned?" Jack restrained himself from looking out one of the portholes. "They can't try a landing from this far out. That's suicide."

"Also known as the Chinese plan," Clegg added, and then snorted at his own joke. Jack had forgotten how predictable Clegg's humour could be. Oh well, if everything went as planned, it was only a week there and back. And if it didn't go as planned, well, Clegg would probably have a joke about that, too.

Winchester shook his head. "It doesn't appear to be going to the Moon. Vector's all wrong."

Jack's "Then where?" was met with just a shrug. Apparently, they weren't getting any more information.

Just before Jack quite formed the thought, Clegg asked it, "Did they just abandon the ISS?"

Again Winchester shrugged. "I don't have the answers. Not yet."

"No, but they do," Jack gestured in the general direction of *Novyy Mir*. "Let's talk turkey."

Winchester opened his mouth to object, but closed it. Clegg nodded his agreement. Jack returned the nod and reached for the communications unit as Winchester handed him an earpiece. Jack tuned to the international band that the ISS normally used to talk to Earth.

"*Liberty* calling ISS... calling *Novyy Mir* ... are you in distress? Repeat, are you in distress?" No answer. Jack tried again, then waited. He tried one more time, "Knock, knock, anybody home?" Jack shouted.

"We're busy! Go away!" A male voice answered abruptly. No matter what Jack tried after that, there was no further contact that day. And they never caught sight of the lander. Wherever it went, it wasn't reflecting sunlight their way.

"At least it wasn't Olga," Winchester offered. "And I guess we know they're still there."

"Yeah, but what are they up to?" Bryan Clegg was well aware of just how hard and fast Jack had clenched at Olga's name. He hoped to change the topic. He failed.

"Olga? You want to talk about her? Now?" Jack sat up as best he could in the restraints, looking over Clegg at Winchester, redness filling his face

"It's not my fault your marriage was weak." Winchester grimaced. "Your wife must've had a reason to distrust you. These things don't happen in a vacuum."

"Stay out of my marriage."

"Or lack thereof?"

"Guys… Russians." Clegg spoke again, reminding them that he was in the middle. "What's going on with the Russians?"

VI

T minus sixty-eight hours

They could see *Novyy Mir* through the view ports. It wasn't close, and it wasn't easy to see, but they could confirm visual contact. But disturbingly, the Moon was looming large in their windows.

Time was running out.

Bryan Clegg spent most of the morning talking to ground control, going over figures repeatedly. "Yep, we'll intercept them in about forty-five minutes, three hours before lunar insertion."

"Are they still going for an insertion? They jettisoned their lander."

"I don't know. It looks like it." Clegg glanced out the viewport at the ever-increasing *Novyy Mir*. "Maybe you should ask them."

Jack nodded at that. It had been a day since he'd tried to talk to them. This time, he got Olga Krenchova almost immediately. "Have you come to relive our glorious past, my sweetheart?"

"Not funny, Olga." It was an unencrypted channel. Not only

would their governments be listening in, but so could anyone with the right radio equipment. These transmissions showed up on podcasts with an annoying regularity.

"You haven't come to embarrass us?" Olga's disembodied voice had a way of asking rhetorical questions that created the perfect image of her cocking her head with a slight turn as she spoke.

"I've come with air, food, and water." Jack tried not to sound either cocky or apologetic.

She knew exactly what to ask. "And how many guns?"

"Just one." Jack felt more than saw Winchester's twitch at that. Too bad. Only the truth would fix this situation.

"And what of that one gun?"

"I'm willing to surrender the gun to you. But I keep the bullets." There was silence on the other end. "Olga, don't make me hard-dock, please. You know I'm crap at that, and God knows what kind of problems I could cause trying to manoeuvre around all the extra rigging you've added."

Even as he said it, he could imagine mission control wincing. An American astronaut admitting less than perfect skills: Another podcast quote for infamy.

"So, you need Russian help?" Her voice almost contained a chuckle.

"Always," he smiled. She was going to acquiesce; he knew it. Jack nodded to his team members, start the docking process.

"Not so fast, not so fast," Olga's voice came as soon as Clegg had fired the first RCS. "A girl doesn't let just any boy dock with her."

Jack sighed, frustrated. He thought, but didn't dare say, Enough with the sexual innuendoes, you crazy Russian. Even as they needed him, they needed him to be seen needing them more right now.

Russian pride was such a crazy thing to navigate.

"Right," he sighed, "guide us through your modifications and we'll dock at the international port."

T minus seventy hours, nine minutes

Liberty soft-docked successfully with *Novyy Mir*. The two groups met each other warily as the hatch popped. Jack slowly raised two zip-locked bags. One had the gun, the other the bullets. He handed the gun to the nearest Russian and sent the bullets back down to Winchester. That seemed to lighten the atmosphere, although that famous Russian wit was notably sour.

Next came the supplies; food, water, air, enough to get them all home, all passed through the tiny airlock. Then came restarting the international side of the ship. The stench, after only five days, was already abrasive. Lastly, came the hard part: talking.

"Why did you jettison your lander?"

"We sent it to the Chinese, as a present. You know they had a fire?" Jack shook his head and looked at Winchester, who seemed surprised, whether that was an honest reaction or not. "No? Da, they stopped it, but a lot of their oxygen burnt. We sent them some air and some vodka. Did you bring vodka?"

She saw the negative before he replied, "Ah, Americans. You brought guns, but not vodka, because *alcohol* is dangerous."

"But the Chinese should make it home." She continued, "Out here, we help each other. We give them air; you give us air. We give them vodka, you give us ... What? Tang? I hate that crap. You don't know how to live."

Jack was mulling over the implication that the Russians had given away air, had therefore already decided to let his crew dock before they jettisoned the lander, would in fact need them if they wanted to survive.

Before he could formulate a response that incorporated

indignity, resignation, and inevitability...Bryan Clegg drifted over.

"I've been talking to…" Then he pointed, "This guy. Can't pronounce his name. We've got about one hour until we need to burn the remaining boosters on the ISS to take us…"

"… On *Novyy Mir*!" Olga interjected.

"… On whatever … to give us our slingshot home. I've done the math and so has… he. It matches. We can ride this thing the whole way back."

"Sasha," Olga called to the Russian that Clegg had been working with. "Do you concur?"

He nodded.

"Sasha?" Clegg scowled. "That's not the name he gave me."

"You're not a friend," Olga explained. "Not yet anyway. Although you are cute."

"And once we get back?" Jack asked Clegg, waving off Olga's attempts to bait a reaction from him or Clegg.

"We won't be able to put her into LEO. There's no way. But our capsule can take everyone down safely. There are four Russians and we have seven seats. Maybe we can commit the station to a slingshot back this way if there's another crew that can come up, but more likely, we'll lose her forever."

"Ok," Jack looked around wistfully. It was old, this cramped station, and near its end of life anyway, but this was a hell of a way to lose it. People would be pissed. Jack waved Clegg away. "Just get us home."

"Excuse me!" Olga brought her face uncomfortably close to Jack's, her odour reminding him that the reclamation units were still offline. "Who put you in charge?"

"My government." Jack tapped the flag patch on his shoulder.

"Well, my government put me in charge, and those are my Angaras."

Jack rolled his head three different ways, trying to relieve the building tension in his neck. "My mistake. Clegg, get the lady's permission first, then do it."

VII

The news arrived not long after *Liberty* had docked with *Novyy Mir* Two Russians would join the American mission to the Moon next year, making it an international space effort: Two young Russian women with four older American men, in a mission set to last twenty-three days. The Russians were guaranteed to beat both the Chinese and the Indians to the Moon.

McMurty's last comment had been, "Tell Clegg I promised him that we'd find a peaceful solution. We did. Now come on home."

Not everyone found the message satisfying.

"Two Russian women? Oh God, the Americans don't stand a chance," Winchester muttered under his breath.

"In spite of what you told the world, we survived just fine in similar circumstances." Jack admonished Winchester, who just shook his head and floated away.

His aimless drifting took him toward the Russians. Olga looked up, a smile on her face.

"Oh, here he comes! Lover boy! You arranged for us to spend more time together! This makes me happy."

Jack snapped his head up, ready to demand that Olga stop teasing him about that stupid rumour. Instead, he was met with Kevin Winchester's crimson face militantly refusing to make eye contact with anyone.

"What?" Olga drifted over and taunted Winchester's angry

visage. "No kisses?"

"Wait, wait, wait! You and Winchester? But he…" Jack made finger motions between himself and her. "He made the rumour about us."

"Da, covered his transgression by creating yours. You are surprised? Why? It's what I would have done. It makes me love him more."

"Shit! They wouldn't have let him come if they'd known that." Jack felt defeated. All along he'd had grounds to disqualify Winchester from the mission, if only someone had known.

"Yes, they would have, because they do know, and they did send me." Winchester replied.

It took a moment for Jack to unpack that. Then he appraised Winchester with new eyes. "Wait, you weren't the stick. You were the carrot."

Jack didn't add, for a lovesick cosmonaut, because, well, they had the return trip to get through. Winchester shrugged, not looking happy with his new role.

Olga made tsk-tsk noises and smiled distantly, "I've seen the Moon. I'm bored. Take me home, boys. Oh, and turn on those damned reclamation systems! I need to wash my body for my lover boy."

Long-Term Storage

Everyone knows where the answers are – at the event horizon. Hawking radiation retains all information. All you have to do is go get it…

Bold and desperate peoples, attempting to rewrite their history, often tried, and repeatedly failed.

The crew of *Hawking's Hope* had a different plan. Don't try to capture the information, try to join it: Immortality, a long sleep, until someone else figures out how to retrieve them. So the last humans, fleeing extermination, gathered on one ship, gambling on becoming woolly mammoths revived from extinction.

Whether that ship's fool errand worked, we still don't know. Maybe someday.

Dee for the Win

I

"Sixteen and cocky is a stupid way to die!" Kregger taunted Deacon. "You'll be a two-word headline: Splaaatter ball!"

"Eighteen and forgotten is better?" Deacon shot back. "Who knows, Kregger. Keep playing it safe like that and maybe next time you'll come in third!"

"At least I'll live long enough to have kids." Deacon chuckled at that. Kregger was an idiot. No one would ever have his kids.

Not that Deacon expected to live long enough to have any of his own. If you come from the wrong place, the wrong money (or no money), going out in a big splash might be the best you could hope for, one moment of feeling glorious and righteous.

Growing up around the hydroponic susting communities made for an easy way to achieve that: Slaughter ball! Slaughter ball wasn't about killing. It was, in Deacon's mind, about staring down death longer than your opponents could, so they let you win.

Deacon had just out stared Kregger in a shallow water time trial for their next slaughter ball race. Based on the results, Kregger would get one of the middle posts, Deacon a coveted outside post.

Deacon just hoped the next race would come soon.

Returning his tomb to its cradle, Deacon powered it down and towelled off the excess water that had invariably run in when he'd popped the hatch. Strapping and securing the small, transparent ball, Deacon kept an eye on Kregger.

There just weren't a lot of people that Deacon did trust. Kregger certainly wasn't one of them. There had been his mom… and Jeshnit, and… yeah, well, no one else.

Kregger was leaning against the portal, waiting for Deacon, not out of friendship, but distrust. They'd leave together. Deacon had hoped to get some time tweaking his lanyard, but Kregger's grumblings and repeated, "Come on. Hurry up!" pushed Deacon to rush his warm down.

***

Slaughter ball wasn't an official sport, wasn't sanctioned or monitored by any regulatory body. It was an amateur rite of passage perpetuated by the sons (and lately, daughters) of the susting farmers of the hydroponic harvesting yards.

No one ever got rich working the hydroponic harvesting yards. It was where people falling through the cracks ended up. A susting worker had a career expectance of about twenty years, twenty-five if you were lucky. There were very few old time susters, and none with all their limbs. If the sust didn't get you, the sea creatures or your co-worker's stupidity would.

As the saying goes: It ain't no place to raise a family.

But families happened anyway, and children took their places in the line when it was their time. The younger ones watched as the older ones died. Then they stepped up. Each generation held to the slim hope that they would be the ones to break the cycle. Each generation became jaded as the fatalities grew. Each generation passed without count or notice.

Over the past forty years, the susting farmers of Melakka had slowly developed a sense of community, a pride of achievement. Now there were heroes, names passed down to the next generation. With each running, slaughter ball's popularity grew within the community and eventually outside of it as well.

It was an underwater race, with each competitor locked into a fragile, transparent sphere - a slaughter ball tomb - salvaged from some of the older susting harvesters. Players were identified by the colour of their outfits. Inside each tomb was a "lanyard," a gun-shaped tool that fired an anchor beam for a maximum of five seconds. Then it needed to recharge before firing again. Only a direct hit on a keel would anchor your sphere, and then you could change your direction by twisting or yanking on the lanyard.

The course was unstable, often changing even in the middle of a race. That there could be rapidly moving debris was just another part of the thrill. Posted along what could be expected to be the best paths, there were "keels," large inverted teardrop-shaped balls of wood, that could be used to help you navigate.

The first to get around all the keels and through the course, won. There weren't a lot of other rules.

If, no, when tombs collided, they'd sometimes crack or shatter, and the drivers would die; taking along breathing apparatus wasn't against the rules, but it was considered bad sportsmanship.

You could win by being the fastest. Char Osbaldistan was the speed champ. She was so accurate with her lanyard that if you hadn't fouled her up by the first keel; she was gone. She'd won five of the last seven events she'd raced in. But she didn't race any more, and had moved away. Rumour was that she'd gotten better offers, better uses for her talents.

You could win by being the boldest. Sedge Black was the boldest. He'd thread the smallest gap to get ahead. He'd even swung around the outside of a keel once, taking the two-seventy angle instead of the ninety, getting a slingshot back into the race at a hell of a high velocity. That was the only time that he'd beaten Osbaldistan. But since she'd left, he did have three more victories under his belt.

Or you could win by being the craziest. Deacon Carver preferred the latter. Others called his technique reckless, but he didn't have a high collision rate. He did, however, cause a lot of other players to collide with each other as they tried to get out of his way. So far, Deacon hadn't won any of the eleven races that he'd competed in, but he'd won a couple of heats. And he'd been working on Sedge's slingshot technique a lot.

***

The media in Bahru, the capital of Melakka, had started following slaughter ball, first in small-print columns of sport results collected from around the planet and the empire, then with small recaps of races.

Finally, they'd done a profile of a slaughter ball winner. He'd died the very next race, which cemented the press's attention.

Eventually, they found Char Osbaldistan and turned her into a media darling, the epitome of the oppressed susters: noble of spirit, brave beyond redemption, and damned good at what she did.

Char got a lot of attention, and by Melakka standards, she became famous. But she was nineteen, more than a little too old for the game. So she started running the gauntlet less often, and eventually she escaped.

Deacon Carver, on the other hand, sent daily updates of his practice schedule to every reporter who had ever filed a slaughter ball story. The only thing he wanted was to see his name in print before he died. He was about to turn seventeen. He knew that time was running out for him, too.

Slaughter ball races only run when susting can't be done, when the current is at its heaviest, most erratic. When exactly the current would become unworkable was always an open question. It was a matter of when the natural dam at Gredring would collapse, a semi-annual event, and allow the flow of thicker sleewater to run through the susting grounds. There was little notice of when it would start, but once it ran, everyone knew that it would only run for six or maybe seven hours.

So slaughter ball drivers had to always be ready. There were obvious down times, the months following a damburst, while the natural dam rebuilt itself and interrupted the flow of sleewater until the pressure again beat down the living organism that comprised the dam.

Even when the dam was strongest, the sleewater never quite went away. It always seeped through, always made the current needed for the susts to grow. The mixture of sleewater and seawater were key to sust survival, and sust farming.

Sust farming itself was dangerous. Susts were lethal to humans in their living form, electrical currents ripped through their willowy leaves. The bark of the sinuous branches made pharmaceutical companies rich in its processed form.

So humans farmed in the irregular current, trading off safety for money, wearing just enough gear to keep alive without hindering farming activities, as long as everything went right.

When something went wrong, a twisted current pushed you into a sust tangle, or a predator evaded detection and attacked you, your gear wouldn't save you.

The floating community of Sust Aggregate Community 7 wasn't particularly more profitable than any other community, but a fluke of geography had made it the base for slaughter ball. The best course was under the community. It also made it the home of some of the best slaughter ball drivers. But even slaughter ball drivers have to make a living sust farming, and even slaughter ball drivers aren't immune to predators.

***

The warning alarm went off during Deacon's sleep cycle. He shot out of bed and grabbed a pair of shorts before he hit the door button and broke into a run for the nearest dive platform. Divers would be doing quick ascents to escape whichever predator had triggered the alarm. Deacon, and all off-duty sust farmers would converge at the diving platform, help clear the crowds, sort farmers into hyperbaric chambers, and generally try to save as many coworkers as possible.

More experienced divers would be manning weapons stations to try to keep the predator away from the diving platform and the floating community in general.

It was a frantic fifteen minutes, as they got people onboard until there was no one left waiting. Initial head counts showed three missing. There was always hope that they'd found cover somewhere, waiting it out as the community defences tried to flush out the predator and clear a safe passage. But there was also another possibility.

"Blood in the water," Deacon heard someone shout, as he moved between his assigned hyperbaric chambers, taking attendance through the comms units, helping to discover who among them was missing.

"Clear shot, clear shot, clear shot!" A comms voice overrode all channels. Even as it faded, there was the echo-y twang sound of a lancer firing underwater. "Hit! Hit! Hit!"

"Confirmed, confirmed, confirmed! Predator has been hit! Repeat, predator has been hit." Like everyone else, Deacon was looking at the speaker and counted. He got to five before he felt the faint whump of the lancer charge exploding in its target.

The shared feeling of accomplishment at killing the predator was quickly swept aside by the grim reminder that there was blood in the water. Someone wasn't coming home, and in Deacon's hands was part of the answer as to who.

"Last, as usual!" Kregger nudged Deacon. "Not like it's life or death or anything."

"Gimme me that, you lazy scab!" The emergency manager grabbed the clipboard from Deacon's hands, a continuous stream of disparaging comments about Deacon's work ethic flowed from his mouth.

A quick check against master lists, and three names stood unaccounted for. As per procedure, Deacon and the others took those names back to the chambers and asked if any of them were present in the chamber. In each case, the answer was a bitter 'no.'

When he'd returned with his negatives, Deacon, who had never bothered to train for the Rescue and Recovery team, was dismissed, sent back to his quarters.

When he got to his small quarters, no more than a dining room with a sleep alcove, Jeshnit was there, still there. Deacon had forgotten her presence when the alarm sounded. She had a warm drink waiting for him.

"Well, everything OK?"

"No," His face probably told her before his words. "Three missing. Blood in the water." Jeshnit crossed herself upon hearing that.

"Sedge Black is one of them," Deacon added, sounding forlorn.

"You barely know Sedge, and for sure he doesn't like you. Why the drama over him?"

"I don't know… I guess… I've gotta beat someone. What's the point of winning a slaughter ball race if Sedge isn't in it? Char's long gone. Who's left to beat? Kregger?"

"You're kidding right? Three people may be dead, and you're worried about your racing reputation?" A news blip flashed red on the wall monitor. They both looked. It was an eslem eel that had attacked the farmers. There was one fatality that day, a new farmer named Klari. Sedge and another farmer, Trink, had made it safely to cover on the sea floor below and were now ascending at a proper, slow pace, escorted by armed divers.

Jeshnit turned an accusing eye toward Deacon, "Happy?"

To which he sheepishly nodded.

II

"You can't slingshot." Jeshnit was adamant in her conviction.

"Sure I can. Anyone can," Deacon countered.

"I don't mean it's against the rules. I mean you're not good enough." She was exasperated by Deacon's foolhardiness. He was almost seventeen. It was time for him to settle down and have kids, and if he wouldn't, then she needed to find someone who would. This stupidity had to stop, reason had to prevail, or she had to leave.

"Haha… No one is good enough until they are. You don't get better by not doing."

"No Deacon, but you do get dead by doing." She sat in front of him and started stroking his hair. "Look, the guys your age, they're either married with kids or dead. It's time for you to decide which path are you going to follow?"

Deacon had known that this was coming. It wasn't the first time Jeshnit had breached the topic, but he didn't have an answer, and no answer, in his own mind, was no commitment.

Deacon just wasn't there yet.

He met her gaze, and the biggest, longest, and last argument of their relationship started. It took almost an hour, but it ended with her leaving, and him feeling both angry and, somehow, free.

He looked at the wall monitor. Twenty minutes until shift, not enough time to sleep, but maybe enough for a shower. He grabbed his kit and headed for the communal bathroom, Jeshnit no longer on his mind.

III

It had been months since the last collapse of the dam. Deacon was starting to get antsy about when the next slaughter ball race would be. He kept his tomb in perfect shape, polishing and polishing until his arms ached, always ready to go within two hours' notice, the time it would take to charge the batteries. With each polish, he dreamed of how he'd spend his winnings, what upgrades he'd make to ensure that he kept winning…

When the warning came, Deacon was underwater, hauling mature sust stalks toward the collector bin. He quickened his pace, got his cargo in just in time for the gate, and rode up on a slow line, decompressing properly as he did. He spent the whole forty-minute ride up planning his slaughter ball strategy. It was to be Sedge's last race, the reigning champion and sentimental favourite.

Deacon had every intent of raining on his parade.

The keels were set, the tombs and lanyards powered up. Usually there were eight competitors, but this time there were only six, and only two mattered to Deacon; himself and Sedge. Deacon was stationed on the left edge of the dump ramp, Sedge, second from the right, with a few on either side of him.

As the countdown to drop started, Deacon found himself staring through the tombs at Sedge's bright blue headscarf and jacket.

I wonder what he's thinking.

At five, Deacon tore his eyes off the competition and started positioning his controls. At one, Deacon felt a slight bump on his side. His nearest competitor, yellow in colour, had locked a lanyard onto him… What the …?

At zero, the ramp dumped, and the tombs dropped, but Deacon's tomb was connected to the next one, and they lost momentum as they hit the current. The lanyard turned off, freeing him, but it was too late. The four remaining tombs had a five-length lead. It would take a miracle for Deacon to win now. Bastards!

Deacon felt for the current, sensing that it was deeper than him. He lanyarded his yellow opponent and swung down, inversely pushing the other up, away from the current. Deacon let go almost immediately, using less than a second of power - a five second recharge penalty that he could easily absorb as he felt out this current. He felt the push of the sleewater and tumbled once before righting, the ballast in the bottom of his tomb working with gravity. As he spun, he looked to ensure that he was now out of range of his dastardly opponent.

Ahead, he thought he was gaining distance on the four remaining tombs slightly above him. The keels pulsed red among the bluish discharge of the sust. First keel ahead and down. Deacon watched as they all lanyarded it, swinging down and right, towards a second keel that Deacon couldn't see yet. Deacon followed their lead, biding his time. He knew that he could probably have swung wide on that keel, but there was so much sust in the area that he probably would have lost speed instead of gaining.

Now he was in the same current as all the others, he would neither gain nor lose ground until the next keel. He deciphered the colours ahead of him. Sedge in blue, another in flourescent green, a bright pink one, and one that was some unsportsmanlike dark brown. That'd be Kregger, an old-timer who never amounted to anything, and who thought that wearing dark colours made him cool. Deacon was in bright orange, and there was the yellow competitor somewhere behind him.

Deacon contemplated doing what had been done to him. A lanyard shot on Sedge would pull Sedge out of the group. Deacon wouldn't overtake him, but the other three would. Still, that didn't seem fair, so Deacon held off.

Instead, he needed to outsmart these guys. There were only four keels on this course, and they were approaching the second. As the four tombs ahead of him jockeyed for the best shot at keel two, they started nudging each other, not enough to be fatal, but enough to slow them down.

Deacon aimed for the bottommost point of the keel, below the paths the others appeared to be taking, and held his lanyard steady, waiting to get close enough. Just as he was going to fire, another lanyard beam hit the same spot. Sedge's tomb slid down below the others and began his turn. Deacon fired anyway. Damn Sedge for the same idea and execution, but still, Deacon got a cut on the remaining three tombs.

He was still behind Sedge, heading for keel three, but he was slightly ahead of the rest. Incrementally, he knew, he could win this, as long as the course was long enough. He just had to act before Sedge, be a bit bolder than him. Even as he locked onto keel three, he also saw that keel four and the finish line were very close.

Damn, it was a short course.

The current took a bounce down and back up, and now the fourth keel was ahead, but slightly above them. The purple glow of the finish line was too close. A quick glance showed that no one else would be close enough to matter. It was a two-man race.

He knew what he'd do in Sedge's place, fire his lanyard toward the bottom quarter, not leaving Deacon enough room to come under him. Deacon needed a second strategy, a plan that would give him speed enough to win and defeat Sedge's strategy… a sling shot!

Rolling his tomb slightly to the right, Deacon lined up his shot. He saw Sedge's lanyard connect with the keel exactly where he'd expected. That committed Sedge to his strategy. Now for Deacon's.

It took three quick firings to perfect a sling shot; the first to pull you out of the current, the second the start you on your fresh course, the third and longest to fling you back into the current at your new trajectory. Deacon's first shot hit the outside of the keel, above Sedge's. It didn't matter; they weren't going to collide when they were going opposite sides of the keel. He quickly flexed once and released, setting his second shot a little above and further around the outside of the keel. Another flex, release and the third shot, same latitude on the keel, but further around. A sharp, sustained tug on that lanyard, and Deacon released.

He re-entered the sleewater current with a jarring thump, and rocketed forward, his tomb hitting the side of Sedge's. There was a sharp ringing noise, but it didn't linger, which probably meant that the tombs were both still intact.

They were at the finish line: a beep in Deacon's ear indicating that he had crossed. He looked around quickly. Both his and Sedge's tombs had been caught in the nets and were being pulled toward the landing ramp. He couldn't tell which one was further in front. It didn't help that the tombs both slipped down the netting, obscuring their initial points of impact.

Deacon cracked his tomb's hatch and jumped out. There was already a crowd around Sedge, some slapping him on the back, but Deacon had seen no results yet. They seemed to think that Sedge had won, but Deacon wasn't ready to concede.

Sedge glared at him through the well-wishers as the overhead screen showed the finish. It had been close, but Deacon's tomb had clearly been a few centimetres ahead when they reached the line.

The crowd hushed as the screen presented Deacon's profile as the winner. The same group that had crowded around Sedge pointedly did not come over and congratulate Deacon. They simply dispersed, bottles of victory ale hastily re-corked.

When they finally loaded the last tombs onto the ramp, Deacon went over to confront the yellow racer, a first-timer named JayJay, for nearly costing him the race. The kid didn't care. He was bouncing off the deck for having simply survived his first slaughter ball race. And of course, Sedge and the other racers, the same people who wouldn't acknowledge Deacon, came over to congratulate JayJay on the finish.

Deacon immediately broke away and lodged a protest against JayJay, but to no avail. No one died and the outcome of the race was not affected by JayJay's actions, so the judge's instant verdict was that no response was needed.

Deacon shook his head. Damn right a response was needed. He had to settle for punching JayJay in the face. That shut the brat up. Bloodied his mouth, too.

Approaching the podium, the winner's podium, not the participant's podium that he usually stood on, Deacon felt insulted, frustrated, unappreciated. He'd won. Fairly. In spite of foul play. Losers, he thought as he walked past the second and third place finishers, Sedge and Hartley. He stood tall, as tall as he could, given his height, and accepted the medal. He held it aloft, shaking it victoriously, to muted applause.

A frown creased his brows.

He'd never heard such a quiet acknowledgement of a new champion. People even seemed to be shushing others who started cheering. Screw 'em, he thought, as he stepped off the podium. Sore losers.

He saw Jeshnit in the crowd, tried to get to her, but she was gone before he could reach her.

IV

Deacon's alarm went off, and the national news broadcast filled his room, already in progress.

An angry man was speaking. "…this attempt by the Tripartite Alliance to take over the Non-Aligned Territories will not stand."

The newscaster's much calmer visage filled the screen. "We'll keep you posted on developments related to this story. And finally, some local news. A slaughter ball race was run under Sust Aggregate Community 7 last night. Defending champion Sedge Farline was barely defeated by the newcomer, Deanna Carver. Some racing irregularities were reported, but the result stands. Miss Carver was not available for comment, and we are told that she has retired from slaughter ball racing. Now for corrections from yesterday's newscasts…"

What? Deacon looked at the screen, perplexed. Retired? She? What?

Deacon's second alarm, the five minutes to check-in warning, brought him back to the present. He grabbed his coveralls and bounced out into the hallway. He could call the news station on the way. He got on the tram, squeezed past an old lady into a seat in a corner, and placed his call.

Even before the call connected, he was aware that others were watching him, snickering, hiding smiles. This had to stop. He was the winner. Where was the respect?

"News Central. How may I place your call?"

"I'd like to report an inaccuracy in a news story."

"Yes sir, I'll send you to Billing."

"Billing?" he asked, even as the call connected.

"Yes, this is Billing. How may I help you?" Deacon was aware that everyone around him could hear his side of the conversation, and those closest might even be able to hear both sides.

"I want to report an inaccurate story in your broadcast. Is this where I do that"

"Yes, sir, which story?"

"The one about the slaughter ball race last night. You got the name and gender of the winner wrong."

"Let me check." As the line went on hold, the tram pulled into the next station. Sedge and Kregger boarded, as they often did. Deacon waved a distracted hand. They didn't wave back, but the movement of boarding passengers pushed them back to his part of the tram.

The operator came on and read the transcript of the story to Deacon, then asked what the inaccuracies were. "The winner's name was Deacon Carver - D-e-a-c-o-n space C-a-r-v-e-r."

"No sir, the winner was a woman named Deanna Carver. That has been verified."

"You didn't verify it, because I'M THE WINNER! I KNOW MY NAME!" Deacon's shout drew far too much attention on the tram. People were starting to get fidgety.

"I'm sorry," there was a slight pause, "ma'am? What was your name?"

"Deacon Carver - D-e-a-c-o-n space C-a-r-v-e-r. And it's not ma'am, it's sir!" The old lady sitting opposite Deacon stood up and moved away. There was a pause as other passengers waited to see if anyone would sit there. Kregger did.

"I'm sorry ma'am, we don't have any record of you in Billing."

"What's Billing got to do with this?" Deacon's exasperation was filling the whole tram now. "Why do you keep calling me ma'am?"

"You wanted to buy a correction to a news story, didn't you?"

"No, I want you to do your job and tell the actual news!" The old lady sitting next to Deacon got up, not wanting to be around that much vitriol. Sedge sat down beside Deacon, nudged him gently with his elbow. Deacon looked up.

"Ma'am, that's not how it works…"

"Call me ma'am one more time…"

Kregger mouthed more than spoke the words, "Hang up. Call back."

Deacon exhaled loudly. "Hold please," he told the Billing Department.

What a mess. He shook his head. He took a moment to check that he wasn't near his stop yet before turning his attention to the other two racers.

"What?" He looked back and forth between Kregger and Sedge.

"Think about the race last night, mate. Did you really deserve that win?" Sedge started calmly, but Kregger was having nothing to do with calm.

"You almost killed Sedge and Hartley." Kregger shouted in Deacon's face, spittle popping like fireworks in random directions. "That stupid split-swing move you did at the fourth keel sent Trarian flying off course. She almost hit an anchor. But all you're worried about is your name in the press. Well, screw you and screw your vanity. We bought the media coverage of this race. They'll never say your name correctly. Not unless you're willing to spend all the prize money on one newscast."

"So," Sedge cut in waving Kregger off, "You gotta ask yourself. What's more important? Upgrading your tomb or hearing your name on the news?"

Deacon knew that he didn't always control his anger well, but now he felt a rage he'd never felt before. They would never let him win again. He'd be marked. There'd always be a JayJay willing to break the rules just to win favour with the big boys. There was no way to win: Not in slaughter ball, not with Jeshnit, not in this mess: Not for Deacon.

The only question was, what was the best way to lose?

"Hi, Billing?" He spoke into his earpiece, his eyes locked on Sedge. "I have two corrections to that story. First, the name is Deacon Carver - D-e-a-c-o-n space C-a-r-v-e-r and secondly, I am male. But the retirement part is true, you can keep that. You can say that I'm retiring as the first undefeated champ since Char Osbaldistan. Yes, I'll pay."

The Guardian's Keeper

The old lady fought off my mugger.

"He wasn't after your purse, but your wee one."

"Why?" I looked at Liam, sleeping in the stroller.

"Come, I'll show ya." We walked to a part of the park I'd never seen before. Dark trees closing in on us until we reached the riverbank. "Nessy, look."

It rose from the water, the fabled, terrifying beast. Liam gurgled delightedly.

" 'e's yer new guardian." She spoke to the beast. "I'll keep 'im safe til he's old enough."

"You," She spun me away. "We're done with."

. . .

"Then I was here. Please, officer, find my son!"

Graceful Degradation

I

All Jeremy wanted was a copy of the 312th playing of Emma Mac's *Nights in Bangalore*. Jeremy hated the song, hated everything it made him feel. But he needed it, had to find it; it was a part of Sara.

***

Sara's funeral had been traumatic, of course it had. His wife was dead. For the funeral, he wanted to play their wedding song, *Nights in Bangalore*. For the wedding, they'd bought a new copy so that they'd have the full version for the big day. By then, the song had been a minor hit, and when it played on the radio, it tended to be around the 200th playing.

Sara had been obsessed with the song, she thought it epitomized one of the most graceful degradations she'd ever heard. She could guess within ten plays or so how many times the song had been played, just by listening to how the keyboards disappeared over time. To Jeremy, it just seemed like they were present one listening, then he didn't notice them anymore.

Nights in Bangalore degraded so gracefully, it had swept the awards in the technical category. At the 200th playing, it still sounded optimistic, but was starting to show a moodiness that wasn't apparent in the previous listenings.

The whole time Sara had been battling cancer, she'd gone back to the song as a touchstone, a promise of hope denied. It made her weep; it made her peaceful somehow. The night she died, she'd listened to the 312th playing. There wasn't much of the song left by then, the voice was fading; the slapdrums were intermittent, if poignant, and a faded acoustic guitar was all that was left of the original wall of sound.

***

"Get out! Don't come back!" A needless shove as Jeremy left the store, demonstrating for any witnesses that the shopkeeper had rejected Jeremy's presence. They could testify to that in court if needed.

A few people stared, puzzled looks. Not many people got thrown out of music shops. Jeremy pulled up his list. It was already fading. He'd have to hurry to the last few if he didn't want to have to recreate the list. Not that there were a lot of music shops left to try.

A short taxi ride later, and he found one last shop. It was dark, around the corner from a major thoroughfare, a lot less foot traffic than the previous one.

Jeremy wondered if that was good or bad.

He walked into the dank, dark shop. It didn't have the current top forty hits splayed across its walls the way others did. It didn't have the usual banter playing as people argued over the best version of a song.

Instead, there was a young girl playing an old upright piano. A piano! Those were rare, possibly illegal.

Jeremy listened, transfixed. He hadn't heard someone actually play music for a long time. It sounded like a current song, maybe Helia's *Try Me*. He looked, but of course there wasn't any sheet music, no note papers. She was playing from memory, or ear.

He didn't want to interrupt but, "excuse me?"

She started. "Oh, you scared me. I didn't hear anyone come in."

"I… I'm sorry. I'm looking for a song. I was hoping you could help?"

She stood up, and Jeremy felt a pang of guilt. She wasn't much more than a child. What he was about to ask of her would be a serious crime. Maybe he should just leave her alone. But, a deep part of him replied, she plays music by ear.

"Do you work here?" She nodded. She was wearing a name badge - Michelle, it said. "I… my wife passed away a year ago. She … she was listening to *Nights in Bangalore* when she died." The girl crossed herself, nodded. She'd heard of the song. "I'm looking for a copy of the song, the 312th playing, or 311th so I can play it at her memorial next week."

"*Nights in Bangalore*? Emma Mac? Old song?" Her voice trailed off as she walked to a bin filled with the small discs music invariably came on, each with a number scrawled on it. She flipped through it. "A song that old, you rarely find anymore. But if there was a re-issue…"

Jeremy could see that she was looking up in the distance, the look of someone engaging in a cortical net search.

Again, he felt a pang. She was leaving a trail, she could be found later.

"Nope, sorry." Michelle turned back to him.

"Just as well." He sighed.

"Look," she had a cautious expression on her face, "I know people. Give me your contact. No promises, I'll see…"

He hesitated for a second, but it was for Sara. He gave her his contact and turned to leave.

As Jeremy left, Michelle sat down at the piano again and started playing Try Me again. Jeremy paused at the doorway. Of course, it would sound the same every time she played it.

How odd. How…illegal.

II

Sitting at home, Jeremy took the fading wedding photo out of the fridge. Keeping it cold slowed the fading process, but of course photos are only supposed to last ten years.

Nothing lasts forever: Official government policy. The past is gone, forget it, another policy.

Want to preserve your wedding photos? After a decade, you were expected to re-take them. Unless your partner was dead, then you were out of luck.

"We could retake them?" Sara offered, knowing that a year of chemo and radiation had taken a hard toll on her. He demurred. He didn't want to remember her this way.

In hindsight, he'd been wrong. He cried many nights in bed, realising that every artefact of her existence would expire at some point, that he'd lose her permanently, inevitably.

He opened a drawer in his old desk and pulled out a piece of paper: blank, fresh and a violation of every memory law.

He'd taught himself how to make it in his basement.

Paper itself wasn't hard to make, per se, but paper thin enough and consistent enough that you could trace a photo through was difficult, and he was proud of the three sheets he'd been able to produce.

By cutting the paper in half, he could preserve at least sketches of six photos of his life with Sara.

***

In the local café, Jeremy bought a short story with his latte. It was 'Thunderstorms over Giverny,' a beautiful story about pretty flowers threatened by a huge thunderhead. By the time Jeremy finished grocery shopping and gone home, the story had already begun to fade.

C'mon, you used to get at least a month out of a story, now they fade immediately? He thought for a moment. He had a bottle of ink in the medicine cabinet, labelled iodine. He had paper. Some of his earliest pieces had been too thick and rough for trace paper, but he'd kept them around.

Jeremy sat down and carefully transcribed the story in its original form, then posted it on his fridge. The next day, the story had morphed, the disappearing parts were apparently timed: now the emphasis had shifted to the inevitability of the flowers' demise.

Jeremy didn't like it, but he copied it down too.

A day later, the story was very short and only described dead flowers. Jeremy hated it, but he wrote it down diligently. He put it up on the fridge with the other two.

On the fourth day, the only words left were, 'Did you enjoy this story?' and a hyperlink that he hadn't noticed before. He wanted to answer, 'no' but worried if he did so, he would attract scrutiny. He went onto the café's feedback page and wrote out a complaint about how quickly the story had faded. But he didn't submit it; that too might be dangerous.

***

Jeremy never told Sara about his secret skills, not until she was dying. Then he'd promised to preserve as much of her as he could.

"Children would have been nice," she smiled sadly. Another regret. Time for everything, but never time for children. He nodded, tears bursting out. Children would have kept a part of her alive. Their little cottage wouldn't be so empty now.

Sara's funeral hadn't quite gone as planned. By the time they'd actually gone through all the rehearsals, *Nights in Bangalore* had passed its 315th listening. It was common for higher numbers to show faster degradation, the signal that this song, too, was ready to be forgotten. There was a huge and noticeable difference between 312 and 315, at least to Jeremy.

He'd been angry at the funeral home for playing it so often before, for not honouring his wish that play 312 be reserved for Sara.

That was almost a year ago. In a few days, there would be a memorial for her, the uncapping of her headstone: The last celebration of her existence before she too faded away forever. Already friends were wondering when he'd take a new partner. Time to move on, they said. Nothing lasts forever. Not even memories.

Jeremy wanted 312 for that day.

III

Jeremy received a discreet post in his eyebox. It told him that a shop had found the song he was looking for, without going into details. This wasn't uncommon. People often tried to track down specific points in a song's degradation, to hear and memorise some specific little nuance.

But he hadn't given his contact info to anyone except young Michelle, who'd been particularly sympathetic to his situation.

Jeremy realised that the eyebox message was already starting to fade. He quickly memorised the address - oddly, it differed from the store. He noted the time to arrive. There was no return contact, or it had been the first thing to fade.

Dammit!

The message faded to white, closed, and was gone.

***

This was ridiculous, he thought as he stepped out the door. Even if this were real, why would these people do an illegal thing for me? Jeremy suddenly had a thought. He ran into the bathroom and grabbed the bottle marked 'iodine' from the cabinet.

The spring tulips had all closed for the night, protecting their petals from the still nippy April air. Overhead, distant lightning cast shadows all around Jeremy. He counted to twenty-five before he heard the thunder - still a long way off.

He was sure he had memorised the address correctly, but it turned out to be an old Scottish Rite church, still well-kept and functional as a food distribution centre. Religion, too, was to be forgotten. Probably most people who saw the words carved on the masonry wouldn't have a clue as to their meaning.

The food distribution centre was closed for the night, the gravel parking lot empty, but there was a light shining over a side door sunk a few steps into the ground. Jeremy knocked on the side door.

The young girl, Michelle, opened the door and waved him in. Steps led down to a well-lit basement, windowless. Jeremy undid his overcoat and hung it on the landing wall next to others. Looking into the room, he could see maybe a dozen people, all younger than him.

"Right? Who's this?" A burly young man challenged Jeremy as soon as he entered the room proper.

"He's ok, Duncan. He's with me."

"You don't have the best record, lass." Duncan turned full on to Jeremy, "Oy, you a cop? Come to arrest us?"

Jeremy sighed, reached into his vest pocket, and pulled out the bottle. "See this?"

Everyone backed away, including Michelle. "Poison?" She sounded betrayed.

"Ink… here," He uncapped the bottle and walked over to a wall. He dipped his finger in the ink and started writing in broad strokes. The words 'This is writing' soon covered a span of the wall.

"Oy! Are you one of those graffiti artists?" Fear had replaced bravado in Duncan's voice. Graffiti, or any writing in public, was an immediate death sentence, delivered on the spot. "Trying to get us all killed, are ya?"

"I'm a … man who lost his wife. I want to preserve her memories. She," a nod toward Michelle, "says you can help."

Even as he put the ink bottle away, others ran up and scrubbed at his words, making a huge stain on the wall, but at least making the words mostly indecipherable.

"Coffee…" He advised, "coffee will clean the ink, water will clean the coffee. It'll leave a faint stain, but no real evidence." People scurried. The coffeemaker was brewing a new batch in no time. In the end, the stain was huge but even and random, an inexplicable smear along the wall.

"Here." Michelle handed Duncan a small disc as the panic over the scrubbing subsided.

"*Nights in Bangalore?*" Duncan smirked. Whatever credibility Jeremy had achieved with the ink had taken a setback. "Usually it's old rock, The Who, Queen, the Stones' *Gimme Shelter*, stuff like that."

"It's what my wife was listening to when she died." That got Duncan's understanding, if not sympathy. "Can you degrade it to 312, then lock it?"

"Yeah mate, then we never see you again, understood?"

***

Jeremy put the little disc in his music box and listened. It really wasn't the best version of the song. In some ways, 315 had actually been better, now that he thought about it. But authenticity counted.

This is what she heard last. This is what I'll remember.

He put the song on repeat and sat at his desk.

He'd been waiting for this moment to trace the wedding photo. He'd learned from his mistakes with some of their other photos. This one he'd be sure to make perfect. He carefully taped the tracing paper over the picture, adjusted the light so his hand didn't cast a shadow, and began lovingly outlining Sara's face.

At some point, the rain started thudding on his windows, giving the night a deeper sense of intimacy. The light flickered once or twice. The song played on. Rolling waves of thunder passed overhead and were gone.

Then the thunder was back again…

No, not thunder. A knock.

It repeated, rhythmically. Someone was at the door, in the rain. Jeremy opened the little viewing gate and saw two policemen. Behind him, the song played on. He hoped it didn't end and repeat while they could hear. He hoped if it did, they couldn't tell that it didn't change. He hoped…

"Sir, we believe there is the commission of a crime occurring. We are opening the door now." The door unlocked at their command and pushed against Jeremy, motorized hinges gently but firmly, forcing him backwards. The first police officer to enter stood in front of Jeremy and pointed to the music box. "There!"

The second officer pushed past and hit eject. He held up the small disc. "Your music box reported you were playing locked music."

"It's the version my wife was listening to when she died," Jeremy offered weakly. Their stances softened noticeably. Then one glanced at the desk.

"Drawing on photographs? Paper? Ink?!" Jeremy sensed more than saw the other officer draw his weapon. "What do you have to say about this?"

"It's my wife! Pictures of my wife! I need to preserve them! She's gone… Please…." Tears welled in Jeremy's eyes.

"Yeah, and this?" The second officer's weapon was tapping the stories on the fridge door. "More paper, more writing. I remember this story; my daughter bought it last week at a coffee shop. She thought it was beautiful, the way the story degraded. You gonna tell us that's for your dead wife, too?"

Jeremy shrunk, head down, defeated. They wouldn't

understand. They couldn't.

"Three counts of writing; What? Four, no five, counts of drawing," The officer counted the tracings taped on the wall, "Illegal paper; Illegal ink; Locked music. Before we take you in for interrogation, do you have anything to say for yourself?"

Jeremy could feel the breath fighting to get into his lungs, could feel the wracked tightening of his chest as his heart rebelled.

Jeremy himself would be facing life in prison, alone with nothing to do but degrade gracelessly, slowly forgetting his Sara. There would never be a memorial service for her. No pictures, no song. Nothing would exist to commemorate her life and their love.

Then he locked on one word: Interrogation. They'd want to know where he got the music. They'd want Duncan and his crew. They'd want young Michelle and her beautiful, never-changing piano music.

How many people would suffer because Jeremy got caught?

Sara, I'm sorry.

"I … have a confession. I … wrote graffiti this afternoon," he whispered.

"Thank you for your honesty, citizen." The voice was calm, almost caring, as the officers stepped back to get out of each other's line of fire.

Jeremy closed his eyes and clung to the memory of Sara one last time.

My First Cosplay

This should be a great night!

Human Cosplay is new to my species. Dressing up in another being's guise is incredibly empowering. It's almost as much fun as making the costume.

Entering the bar, everyone notices my impressive appearance. I must have done well to draw such immediate attention.

There are my co-workers, at the back: the cool crowd, finally accepting me.

"Dreegli, what have you done?" Cute little Shrel asks, exasperated, eyes wildly tracing the blood dripping down my sides.

"I … came as a Human?"

"You're supposed to emulate them, not kill one and wear the carcass."

"Oh…"

Death vs Taxes

The Grim Reaper has been summoned by angry young girls looking for vengeance. He's been summoned by rich old men looking to make a deal. He's been summoned by apprentice witches foolishly trying to prove their skills to peers.

He'd never previously been summoned by the Internal Revenue Service. The novelty of it was enough to ensure he answered.

***

The door of the interview room slammed shut. The far seat was suddenly occupied by his large, dark bulk.

"I was summoned?" The Grim Reaper looked, well, not up, because even seated he was as tall as the one standing in front of him. So he looked … out … with his glowing red eye sockets at … a newly minted agent of the IRS. The agent looked a little embarrassed at how loudly the door had shut.

"You were. Thank you for appearing." The agent sat down opposite the Grim Reaper. A stack of files sat on the desk. The Reaper had been aware of them, but hadn't felt curiosity. It wasn't part of his makeup.

The Grim Reaper pushed the reconstructed summons-to-appear toward the agent. "I don't appreciate the method used. A confetti gun loaded with a shredded summons, hooked to the heart monitor of a terminal man? There was a lack of grace, of style. Uncouth, one might say."

"It touched you. You were served. That's the law. Shall we begin?" Agent Healey turned on the voice recorder. "Your name, for the record, is the Grim Reaper?"

"Yes. And what shall I call you?" The Reaper saw the clip-on name tag. "Ah, yes. Investigator Chuck Healey. Tell me about your family, Investigator Chuck Healey…"

"Personal questions will not be tolerated."

"Nor answered, I presume." If the Grim Reaper could change facial expressions, that tone would have had a Machiavellian smile attached to it. As it was, the Reaper had to settle for its usual fixed grin. "Do you feel fear?"

***

In the observation room, connected by cameras, but safely separated by two floors and many doors, observers were getting worried.

"He's losing it." One agent whispered.

"This could be so bad," said another. "This was such a mistake."

"Just wait. Have faith." The focus technician replied. "All the parameters are within the range of normal."

***

"Intimidation will not be tolerated," Healey continued, just a slight hint of sternness edging in the voice. "Do you have a fixed address?"

"No. Do you?"

"Irrelevant." Healey, unfazed by the Grim Reaper's stare, flipped open a legal pad. "On the street, they call you 'Death'?"

"They do?" The Grim Reaper sat up straighter, as if that were possible. He had not heard this before.

"Yes," Investigator Healey paused. Every response had been anticipated, practiced, scripted - except that one. How to go forward? Healey read the Grim Reaper's presumed biography, "You are a member of a gang called the Four Horsemen — "

"I am?"

"Yes, the Four Horsemen of the Apocalypse." The Grim Reaper just shook his head. "War? Pestilence? Famine? Are none of these familiar to you?"

The Grim Reaper kept shaking his head. "Words. Nouns? Nothing more."

"Oh come, everybody's heard these stories."

"I haven't."

Healey nodded. This was going to be more challenging than expected. The agent scribbled a note on the legal pad, knowing the observers would be able to read it. The Grim Reaper leaned over, curious to see what Healey had written, but the agent pulled an arm around, shielding the notes from the Grim Reaper's view.

"Do you mind?" Slight indignation crept into Healey's voice. Then the agent straightened up, turned to a fresh page on the legal pad. "The quicker we start, the quicker we can finish. Do you know why you are here?"

"Of course. I believe I know better than you do."

"Fine. The charges that are being investigated are that you have been complicit in tax fraud by participating in assisted suicides at optimal times for tax purposes. Do you understand?"

"I've..." The Grim Reaper paraphrased, "killed people so that they could pay less tax?"

"Exactly"

"Do dead people come back to life?"

"I could ask you that, but from my understanding, usually no."

"So, how is dying in any way a tax advantage to a human?" The Grim Reaper had never paid much heed to taxes. He was aware of the saying Death and Taxes, but he hadn't known that it meant him, specifically. Now that he thought about it, it seemed so odd, conjoining a recurring event with a once in a lifetime encounter.

Healey, falling back on training protocols, shrugged off the Grim Reaper's question.

"Let's talk about," Healey pulled down the top case file, "Mabel Huffinper. Do you know that name?"

"I don't remember names, per se." Healey opened the file and showed the Grim Reaper a picture. The shake turned to a nod. It had been a nice private care room in a very large manor.

"She died December 31, 2023," Healey summarized. "A day later and her estate would have been taxed at seventy-five percent. Instead, her estate paid only fifty-five percent. We lost a lot of money because of that one day's difference. Tell me, was she alive when you arrived, Mr Death?"

"They're all alive when I arrive. Otherwise, I would not be needed. And it's Reaper."

"Sorry, Mr Reaper." Again with the scribbling of notes, "So, you admit to killing Mabel Huffinper? In aiding and abetting tax fraud?"

"I admit that I did my job. I am unaware of such things as tax fraud."

"Ignorance of the law is no excuse for breaking it, Mr Reaper," Healey chastised.

Healey paused, changing tack to a more conciliatory tone. A hand reached out and patted the Grim Reaper's digits. "This doesn't look good for you. At this time, I am obliged to advise you that you are allowed legal counsel. Would you like to call a lawyer or have a court appoint one for you?"

"I know no living lawyers. Although I've met all the greats," The Grim Reaper chuckled, "in passing."

"Please stop trying to intimidate me. It will not work."

"I'm not trying to intimidate you." Death slowly turned his red gaze straight into the camera mounted above the locked door.

***

In the crowded observation room, there was panic.

"Why's he looking at us? Is everyone OK? Anyone? Everyone?"

Some discretely messaged family members to ensure that they were safe. A few simply sent "I love you" to those closest to them, last words, if needed. More than one questioned the decisions that had led them into this very room at this very time.

It took a few moments for the sweep of hysteria to pass, but they were all well, give or take a bladder.

***

"Let's talk about Zarinne Shoshanni," Agent Healey continued, unperturbed, as the next case file fell open on the desk, photo ready. The Grim Reaper leaned in at that one. It had bothered him: A reaction to a bee sting, a missing Epipen, her daughter crying for help. It should never have happened. And then the ambulance had shown up, just too late.

Just too late to beat the Grim Reaper.

He had wondered often, should he have waited? But Zarinne had thanked him, even as she had tried unsuccessfully to comfort her daughter, her wispy form passing through the girl twice before giving up.

"It's better this way," she had told the Reaper as she faded.

"Maria Shoshanni saved almost three million dollars in taxes, thanks to you." The Grim Reaper was slower to react to this one. A faint shake of his head started to get stronger. If Agent Healey was aware of the rising anger, he didn't show it. "Sir, honestly, we have no jurisdiction over you —"

"Nor, honestly, I over you," Metaphysical spittle jumped from the Grim Reaper's non-existent lips.

69

"—However, I have been tasked with informing you that estate and inheritance taxes are increasing again this year. Please do not interfere with the government of the United States' ability to collect what is rightfully ours."

"Rightfully yours? You have no rights. I am not responsible for human constructs of obligations and responsibilities." He spoke directly to Agent Healey, leaning in, raising his voice. "And I am not responsible for you."

If Healey felt anything, it didn't show, not even a blink. Nerves of steel.

The Grim Reaper stood tall, polar bear tall, and turned to look levelly at the camera. "I have had enough of this. Summons me again for this foolishness and there will be a price."

And he was gone, leaving a pile of ash where the summons-to-appear had been.

***

In the observation room, cheering broke out, as much from relief as from excitement.

"How the hell did we pull that off?" One of the few actual IRS agents in the room looked around. It was a crowded room, filled with department heads, computer technicians, and soldiers.

"Ssh. Let's get Healey down first."

"How is he?"

"Energy's at thirty-two percent. Lower than expected. Time to recharge."

"Sleep, call it 'sleep'."

A tech opened a line. "Hey, Chuck, well done. It's time to sleep."

On the camera, they watched Healey pull a cable out from under the table, plug it into his fingertip and go to sleep. The quiet expectation within the room finally broke.

"He passed, right? Healey passed?" One of the techs kept asking against the sound of cheering and backslapping.

"Yes, son," Major General Hendricks assured him, speaking loudly enough for all to hear. "Chuck Healey v4.0 passed your Turing test with flying colours."

"Um, sir .... I ... I, I don't think he did." A young woman was waving a printout towards the General.

"Who are you?" The general wanted to freeze her with terror. He wanted to ensure that she knew just how much trouble she was in for raining on his parade.

"I... uh ... I'm the transcriptionist?"

He snatched the papers from her hand, refusing to break eye contact, his icy stare willing her to disappear.

But as he read, realisation dawned on him. They had made a mistake. He felt a dreadful chill only to realize that the temperature drop in the room was real, and sudden. The lights dimmed. his staff were shivering and clouds of expelled breath broke out everywhere.

The transcriptionist hesitantly tapped the printout. "I think we failed." She cringed as she spoke, fearing another outburst.

But the voice that replied wasn't General Hendrick's. It was sonorous; soul-penetrating in a way that the general could only dream his would ever be.

"As do I." was all it said.

The Devouring - A Poem

Saturn's rings showed how bad it would be,
curling, hurling into the gaping maw, consumed by
powers beyond our ken.

By then,
Jupiter was gone, the outer planets too.

The devourer continued, erasing our stepping
stones, our future.

Unexpectedly, messages arrived,
transcribed,
"Don't worry. All will be well."

Asked to explain, it replied,
"I need you, on the event horizon's anterior side."

Hunger unabated, it ate the Kuiper Belt, then
Mars, the Moon, and now Earth.

Our final conversation: "You need us, you
said. Desist, or we're soon all dead."

"Clarification:
I need your planet's mass untainted by foolish
radiation."

The Curator

"We simply don't know what a female of the species looks like." The curator and his director watched the two creatures through the viewing partition. "We've been trying every zoo, biological lab, and eccentric collector we can think of. It's been twenty years. We can't even find another living male, never mind a female, for these two to mate with."

"So that's it, then. When these two die, there will be no more humans." The curator nodded. It saddened him to no end that he would be witness to the extinction of a species, one that might have been a star-faring species, under different circumstances.

"It gets worse. They are both old and not healthy."

"I thought your last status report stated that they should have another ten to twenty years left? They certainly look healthy."

"The shorter one states that the taller one suffers from something called Alzheimers. His body is healthy, but his thought processes are falling apart. It will eventually kill him."

"That is scary." The director moved back from the viewing partition. "Is it contagious?"

"He claims that it's genetic, and that we should not be at risk." The curator paused, not sure what he was getting himself into by stating the next. "But the short one is ill too. He calls it cancer. It's a cell-replication error. Again, not transmittable. We think that we may have a treatment for it soon, but right now, all we can do is treat his pain."

"So they're both dying? The rarest of species in our collection, and both are dying?" The curator could see the director making a decision. "Sell them now to private collectors. Get as much for them as you can, as quickly as you can. They have no value once they're dead."

"But shouldn't we try to save this species?"

"We have tried, by your own account, for almost twenty years and you haven't found a breeding pair. I've been patient, supportive. But now it's about money. We need to fund our work. Selling them will be an unexpected budgetary windfall. Who knows, maybe you'll be able to purchase that female Shledak you've wanted for your other mating experiment."

***

Eong awoke in pain. He felt for his meds, but they weren't where he'd left them. No, he wasn't where he'd left himself. He was somewhere else; a strange room. The walls had flowing colours, vaguely hinting at foliage swaying in the wind. There was a sound of a creek trickling nearby. Bird sounds came and went.

But the bed wasn't nearly as comfortable. And the nightstand with his pain medication was not there.

Looking around, he realized that he was alone. There was no sign of the viewing partition, nor the ever-present curator. Eong had a button that he could push to call the curator if needed.

That, too, was gone.

A panicky moment as Eong spun around, looking for Flip, looking for another bed, some sign that they hadn't been separated. Nothing. Flip was gone. Eong shook his head. Poor Flip. Where was he? Was he alone? How would he adapt to change?

Another bout of pain, deep in his chest, brought Eong back to his own predicament. Where were the pain pills? In the last conversation that he had had with the curator, it had mentioned a possible cure for his lung cancer.

Eong tried to remember anything from his slumber. Had he received treatment? Was there a cure working its way through his body? Sharper, harsher pain answered.

He clutched over and fell back onto his bed, moaning.

***

Flip didn't know where he was when he woke up. He knew that happened sometimes, but this place just looked totally unfamiliar. Usually it looked unfamiliar but his body knew - a hand to the wall here to steady himself as he got up, a glass of water just there…

Nope. No glass of water. No wall, at least not there.

But there were people. Strangers, true, but people still. That was unusual, wasn't it?

Flip got out of bed and looked for his dressing gown for a moment before losing interest in it. There was a chessboard at a table, with glasses, all but one empty, with orange juice. Flip lifted the glass and drank, only to wonder if it was someone else's.

Everyone was looking at him, not angry, but not friendly. He put the glass down carefully. "Hi," he gave a little wave. "Have you seen my dressing gown?"

"Hi Flip, I'm Kata," a young girl sitting at the chessboard said. She couldn't be more than twelve.

"I'm Luica," said another, slightly older girl standing beside her.

"I'm Flip," he knew even as he said it that they knew that already. He looked at the older one. "Your name is?"

"Luica," she smiled patiently. It was what she was programmed to do. Kata echoed her smile. Behind the table, a man watering a plant turned around and also smiled at Flip. "We're your people."

***

"I'm glad they gave us the animatronic creatures to fill out the viewing pen. It would be odd if there were only one human."

"That was a sneaking piece of bargaining you did there, only buying one of the humans, and making it look like we have more. I just hope those machines work well. The curator said they'd been in storage for over a decade."

"Have you been watching the human at all? I'm not sure that it knows that the others aren't real."

***

"You're here for the Shledak? Want anything else? I'm pruning my collection. I'll sell you some pieces cheaply." The curator didn't like this collector. 'Cheaply' would have a steep price, somehow, he was sure. "Hey, weren't you the one who was interested in humans? I think I have one now."

The curator felt both ecstatic and a deep sense of despair. Now? Now? A human, now, after twenty years? Now, after I've sold mine?

The collector flipped through a series of screens in quick succession, then stopped on a live feed. It was a creature of about the right shape, but extremely unkempt, long dirty hair hiding a lot of features.

It looked human. The curator could barely hold back his excitement.

"I speak their language. May I communicate with it?" A nod and a flip of a switch. "Hello, if you understand me, please tell me, are you a human male or female?"

"Female." A voice not used to speaking croaked. Damned the gods twisting in perdition. He'd finally found a human female. Now he had to get the males back.

The collector wasn't stupid - prices rose with demand, and the human was suddenly very much in demand.

The curator could only afford the Shledak or the human, not both. It was an easy decision, his director's orders be damned.

Perhaps he could still save their species.

Perhaps he could unite her with at least one of the males.

***

"Ah, Curator, come to give us our money back, have you?"

The curator was confused. That was clearly not the reason for his visit. "Your pet human died no more than ten days after you sold him to us."

"Did you give him his medication?"

The bot referenced notes. "There is no note here about medication."

"I gave you two medications to give him. One that he could administer daily to control his pain and one that you'd have to give him every five-day for thirty days, to clear out his cancer. I gave this all to your aide at the handover!"

The aide shrugged guiltily. The bot shrugged with even less remorse. The curator fought back a rising hysteria. Why was he doomed to fail in this mission of preserving the humans?

***

"Ah, curator. Welcome! As you can see, we have empowered the entire pack of companions to keep your human happy." The curator studied the tableau carefully. There were at least seven active humaniform figures, gardening, pruning, setting the table. "Perhaps you can help us. The human is just sitting in a chair, inactive, and 'crying' if I understand your notes."

The curator looked again. The human wasn't sitting on a chair, one of the animatronics was; a younger shape. Luica it was, and he appeared to be crying. So did Kata.

By the chair was the large bed, a bundle under the covers in the middle.

"What's that?" the curator asked, fearing that he already knew the answer.

"Ah, one of the companions has ceased to function. It hid under the covers a few days ago and hasn't come out since. We're about to send in a team to investigate."

***

Vlin awoke in a bed in a well-lit room, aware of clean sheets, fresh air. There were animatronic people tending to a table, others tending a flower bed. Even more pulling carrots out of the ground in a mulch garden.

There was a chessboard on the table, with glasses, empty except for one with orange juice. A young female-representation smiled at him. Vlin smiled back, glad even for these fake companions. It'd been decades since he'd seen anything remotely human.

"Hi Vlin, I'm Kata," the young girl sitting at the chessboard said. She handed him the glass of orange juice.

"I'm Luica," said another, slightly older girl standing behind Kata.

Vlin smiled. If he had to live alone, this was the way to do it.

Still, he couldn't help but wonder what would have happened if he'd answered the curator's question truthfully.

Uncertainty Persists

"The world is given to me only once, not one existing and one perceived."

Disheartening uncertainty plagued his dreams: which were real, which perceived?

Indeterminacy was more than a philosophy … they wanted him to love Lucy, not Peppermint Patty Entanglement occurs only over limited distances … the gang didn't wear mittens when skating on the pond The kitten was both dead and alive … but they wanted him to play the piano

Was he Schrödinger or Schroeder? … Beethoven's fifth uncertainty, please.

Heisenberg awoke from his dreams, or were they nightmares? Uncertainty persists!

Note to self: congratulate Erwin.

The Sky Stick

I

Talawahe hated the sky stick. He was the medicine man for his people. He was supposed to be wise. But the sky stick stood as proof of his ignorance. Talawahe had committed his whole being to learning the cycles of life, yet he could not explain this shiny grey thing that dominated their village.

But Talawahe was not alone in his hatred. The stick obeyed no authority. Chief Pedasaya hated it more. When it first arrived, he spent hours shouting orders at it. Now he just spent time staring at it. He feared that its presence made him look weak, opened his people to conquest from neighbours. In fact, those neighbours feared the stick more, and feared that its presence cursed Talawahe's village. No one was going to attack as long as it was there.

The sky stick never moved, but its domed top was clear and you could see into it. That part had circles within circles that reflected your appearance back to you. They would move. And sometimes they would cast a dim red light.

Talawahe was pretty sure that these were eyes, and that the stick could see every way at once.

Talawahe had a hard time explaining how he did not think that the sky stick was alive, and yet he thought it had eyes. Many in his village questioned him, doubted his sanity, doubted his fitness for his role. So late in his career, he was no longer perceived as wise.

As much as their doubts pierced him, as much as the sky stick confounded him, he felt certain that his ideas were correct: The sky stick was watching them, learning.

***

Talawahe had been but a pupa when the sky stick arrived. It came down on a tower of flame and smoke, burning the ground beneath it so deeply that even decades later, nothing grew there. Its arrival had caused much panic. Then, when it did nothing, neither good nor evil, the people slowly started ignoring its presence, an oddity that made their village unique among the neighbouring villages.

Thus it was for the first decade or so.

Their village had not been attacked for many years. When head soldier Selafeha became chief, a few years after Talawahe had become medicine man, he told his council, his people, that it was because the other towns feared his fierce warrior ways.

Talawahe was certain that it was fear of the sky stick that kept others away. The village wasn't seen so much impregnable as cursed.

Selafeha wanted to show his leadership, his distinct militaristic command, by removing the sky stick.

At his behest, they built a pyre around the sky stick and stoked the flames to a heat that threatened to destroy the entire village if the wind took it. In the morning, the rains of autumn washed away all signs of soot, all signs of any effort.

The sky stick remained.

Talawahe preached non-interference. Leave the sky stick alone and it will leave us alone. We can't continue to provoke it. We can't understand what it wants, but it doesn't seem to want to hurt us, he pleaded.

Selafeha called him a fool.

Selafeha was not one to give up. He built a house around the sky stick.

His men first constructed the house in a field, then broke it down to parts so that the complete house could be built around the sky stick in one night, hoping that it would be asleep.

In the night, the chief's men came carrying fitted wooden walls and roof. They quickly built their structure, but as they finished, a wide red light shot along the walls, creating an intense small fire everywhere it touched. Eventually, the house caught fire and burned down.

The sky stick remained.

Selafeha tried again with stone. But the sky stick again used its red light to break down the walls, but this time it was more intense, narrow. Stones fell in carved chunks.

Frustrated at these defeats, Selafeha took a long branch of seasoned wood and struck the sky stick repeatedly. He hit it high; he hit it low. It didn't budge, didn't sway, didn't show any signs of pain.

That was when they learned that you could touch it, but with only so much force.

As Selafeha turned to leave, the red light shot out, piercing his thorax and then his brain stem. Selafeha died that day, and Talawahe swore in the new chief, Pedasaya.

II

Initially, Pedasaya sought Talawahe's counsel, but when it wasn't what he wanted to hear, he then ignored it.

"We should just live our lives. Do not bother it," Talwahe suggested.

"No, this divine stick chose me to be chief of this tribe. We must worship the sky stick," Pedasaya demanded. "You will help me make the rituals that will appease it."

"The one thing I learned from the sky stick and Selafeha was that if you want to appease it, leave it alone." Talawahe would not help design the rituals of appeasement and sacrifice, so Pedasaya continued his predecessor's campaign of belittling and insulting the medicine man.

***

The village walls were just pikes of young tree trunks shoved into rows, strung with reeds. They were barely enough to keep animals out at night. Still, there was a gate, and it was manned.

The gate opened at dawn, closed at dusk. Villagers could come in after dark, but the night guard wouldn't let anyone out.

Talawahe often went out at dawn to collect fresh herbs along the river bank. This morning, there was a procession forming at the gate: four guards and three women. Pedasaya's pregnant daughter, Pedray, among them.

"Good morning, ladies. Where are you off to?" Pedray snorted and turned her back. The other two, her maids, wouldn't be so rude to a medicine man.

"To Wicha village." The younger maid indicated sadness. "To see the medicine man."

"A good medicine man!" Pedray spoke over her thorax.

"Pedray, this is important," Talawahe spoke to her maids as much as to her. "Your mother had pre-hatch death thoughts when she carried you. If you are seeking advice on your egg, you must tell him that."

Another snort from the young woman. Her maids gave clipped bows to Talawahe, the youngest staring longer, bowing a second time. She would remember.

Just after dusk, Talawahe was sitting in front of the sky stick, pounding his herbs, preparing to pickle some for future needs. There was a call from outside the gate.

The night guard opened the gate as Pedray's party returned. Talawahe unfolded his legs and stepped toward them.

"I am sorry to ask when I am unwanted, but did you tell him?" Pedray glared. Her maid nodded. "Did he prescribe pickled ferrian seed?"

Again, the maid nodded. "Did he have any?" Talawahe doubted he would. The village of Wicha wasn't near any ferrian patches that Talawahe was aware of.

Pedray turned at that. "I hate you! Filthy old man. Die already so we can get a real medicine man!"

She scurried away with her elder maid in tow, leaving her guards and the younger maid behind.

"I've been making pickled ferrian seed." Talawahe held up a jar. "It'll be ready by morning. When she calms down, come collect the jar."

Talawahe made a note to himself to send some ferrian seeds to Wicha with simple instructions on how to grow them. No one should be without medicine.

***

There was no immediate replacement for Talawahe. A suitable candidate in the village would have to train with Talawahe, which, his detractors stated, meant that they'd have another damaged medicine man.

No, the village was negotiating to trade for another medicine man from a distant people, one they weren't at war with.

***

"Talawahe, come!" The young maid woke Talawahe in his hut.

"What? What?" He asked through morning fog.

"Pedray is in breach. She speaks death thoughts to her egg!" Talawahe ran after the maid. He didn't need to keep up. It was a small village. He knew where he was going.

"Not him!" Pedray shouted as he entered.

"There is no time to get the man from Wicha," her father replied. "Talawahe, can you save my daughter?"

Talawahe looked her over quickly. She was convulsing, showing pain flinches and flecking. "You haven't been taking the ferrian seeds, have you?"

"Why would I? You tried to trick that medicine man into giving them to me!"

Talawahe shook off Pedray's anger. He turned to Pedasaya. "You've seen this before. Your wife… we didn't have ferrian seeds then."

"Bad choices," Pedasaya agreed. His wife or his daughter, which did he want to save? "I expect better from you now. Save them both, my daughter and her egg."

"I …" Talawahe felt despair. What Pedasaya asked was impossible, but failing to do it would probably also mean the end of Talawahe's life. "I have an idea. I need a stick, painted red. A straight stick."

A guard ran, no, fled the hut to find or make the needed stick.

Talawahe turned to the remaining guards who were hovering near the door, looking for an excuse to be absent but fearing Pedasaya's wrath if they moved outside. "I need a litter for Pedray. We're going to take her to the sky stick."

Talawahe looked to Pedasaya. "You wanted a ritual. Let's see if this one will work."

III

They lay bricks in front of the sky stick. Immediately Talawahe noted the eyes at the top starting to move, to pay attention. Good, you're awake. Now I just need to get you to understand.

They put the stretcher with Pedray in front of the sky stick. A guard handed Talawahe a short red stick. He almost complained that it was too short, but this was a crazy idea, anyway. Who could say that the length of the stick would make a difference?

Talawahe stood between the sky stick and Pedray, looking for the nub that the red beam always came from. He found it. Then he cajoled Pedray into shifting her body so that her lower thorax was in line with the nub.

It was hard to get her to lay still given the pain rippling through her body. "I'm sorry," he said to her as he signalled guards to come over and pin her down. First, they looked to Pedasaya, who gave accent.

"This is crazy," Pedray shouted, "He's trying to kill me! Daddy! Help!"

"I am helping." Pedasaya held Talawahe's eyes as he said it. There was fear, anger, and vengeance marked in the look. Fear above all else. Talawahe nodded fear back.

Talawahe took the red stick. He held it up in front of the sky stick, waving it to make sure the eyes were watching. Then he positioned the short red stick against the nub where the red light comes out, and moved the stick to Pedray, drawing a line on her thorax, just below the egg.

"This is going to hurt," Talawahe summoned as much sympathy as he could, then he tapped the sky stick with the red stick.

The beam came! Talawahe had a microsecond of relief before Pedray's screams of pain shattered the dawn. Talawahe barely got in place in time to catch the egg when it popped out. He spun quickly and handed it to the young maid.

He caught the stunned look on Pedasaya's antennae. No tool in the village could cut open a thorax like that, not without shattering it as to kill the person.

Pedasaya's mind worked quickly. He looked to Talawahe, the thought clear: You've opened a wound, can you close it?

Half way there. Talawahe took a deep breath.

"I need your help now," Talawahe told Pedasaya. "You must push from the top of the thorax, push the wound closed. I will push from the bottom. But whatever you do, don't get in the way of the sky stick!"

One more scream from his daughter and Pedasaya nodded. He placed himself above Pedray and pushed down and back on her upper thorax. He was strong, perhaps strong enough to overcome Talawahe's aged weakness.

They pushed and pushed, closing the gap. As the edges, so cleanly cut, lined up, the red beam returned, wider, fainter, but Talawahe could still feel the heat bleeding off Pedray's Thorax.

Her screaming renewed.

The beam stopped. Talawahe fell back, exhausted, too exhausted to even see if he'd succeeded. Pedasaya collapsed onto his daughter for just a moment, then picked himself up.

The young maid helped Talawahe to his feet. He examined Pedray's thorax. The scar was hot, but it was a scar, not an open wound. He didn't know if her innards had closed up as well. He hoped so.

For now, he had an egg and a living Pedray.

"Do you know what I mean by clay mud?" Talawahe asked a guard, who looked puzzled.

"I do," the young maid said. "It's the grey mud, not the brown mud, on the opposite river bank."

"Yes. I need this. A water bucket's full. You, guard, take this maid. She will show you. You will grab as much as you can carry and run back with it. She will fill the bucket and come back after. I need some now, more later! Go!"

"What…" Pedasaya didn't know how exactly to finish the sentence as the pair ran past the open gate and down toward the riverbank. "What did you do?"

"The sky stick doesn't want to hurt us. It's been observing us for almost my whole lifetime. It knows our cycle of life, what's supposed to happen. I … I hoped that it would help, if it could."

"You are a wise, crazy, old medicine man. I am sorry. I know I misjudged you. I… you are old, aren't you?" Talawahe nodded, still trying to catch his breath from the exertion of closing Pedray. "We need to find you an apprentice."

"If I am wise, may I be eccentric, too?" Talawahe asked between breaths.

"Explain."

"There are no good male candidates for medicine man in this village, but that young maid…?"

"Glardiay?"

"She is intelligent, dutiful, and observant. We could do much worse."

"A medicine woman?" Pedasaya looked at the sky stick, weighing everything that had happened. "Why not?"

Forget Me Nots

Two hundred years ago, we discovered FTL.

A hundred and eleven years ago, we made first contact. War inevitably followed.

Ninety-eight years ago, the remnants of humanity were dispersed among twenty hidden, low profile colonies, none knowing the location of any other, only that they existed.

Eighty-five years ago, omni-directional broadcasts from Earth stopped abruptly.

Seventy-two years ago, catastrophe beacons started broadcasting fallen colonies' epitaphs.

Two months ago, nineteen colonies had been accounted for, destroyed, all but us.

Three weeks ago, something entered our solar system.

An hour ago, our president apologized for failing to save us.

A second ago…

The Mating Rituals of Clouds

I love how the dawn wind tugs you, as it often did, toward the channel that separates Great Britain from Europe. You drift at the same pace as the surrounding clouds, as much one of them as you could ever possibly be. Water vapour fills your waning castellanus, building you taller, wider, blooming from cumulus to cumulonimbus.

Damn, you're good looking.

Of course, altitude is everything. It gives a heady perspective.

You're pleased. This is an opportune moment. Your white filaments fluff out, layer upon layer, shading to grey and beyond, almost to bursting black. But you know you need to hold back, to coax more distance.

It will still be hours before you reach London and can let loose your arsenal.

Darling, time may be yours, but patience is mine.

London, 1914

David Lloyd George answered his summons to 10 Downing Street promptly. Rain be damned. George knew that an early morning summons meant a dressing down, but at least a private one. On the floor of the House of Commons would be a crueller place for this exchange.

"Chancellor of the Exchequer, Austria-Hungary has declared war on Serbia. You said this wouldn't happen." The Prime Minister waved crumpled papers, words not worthy of the ink spilt in their names.

"Yes, Prime Minister."

"Care to explain yourself?" Prime Minister Asquith tossed the meaningless communiques onto a stack on his desk. The papers cascaded down the side to the floor, an avalanche of dead hopes.

"No, Prime Minister."

"I followed your lead, propounding peace at every opportunity. That seems to have failed us. Now what?"

"Listen to me now, Prime Minister, as I shall contradict my earlier inclinations. We must prepare for war, full war, total war, a winner-take-all battle. We must be prepared to sacrifice and to die."

Asquith appeared to deflate. Lately, Lloyd George thought, the Prime Minister had seemed tired, not as robust as his old self. Perhaps he'd been in office too long. He wasn't ready for carnage, not on his watch, not tied to his name.

Perhaps he needed… replacing?

As if sensing the direction of Lloyd George's thoughts, the PM said, "Chancellor, what has gotten into you?"

"Nothing Lord Prime Minister, except the continued safety of his majesty King George the Fifth and all his realms."

***

You have this entire world to roam, but the primates frustrate you, confining their war to such a small space, never moving, never expanding. Still, for four years, you pulled a rich harvest.

Yes, it wasn't as plentiful as it should have been. What was the point of all this industrialisation, if to just sit in one spot taking shots at each other? You need a bigger field to reap, a larger harvest from a greater canvas. You spread out, send cirrus feelers everywhere, scouting carefully.

But these crazy primates don't wait for you. They needed almost no goading, no push, no feedback through the spores.

Russia is in turmoil, Japan has plans. China is ripe for the taking. Within a few years, they were at it again, and much bigger: a war throughout the northern hemisphere, complete with delicious aerial battles, startlingly violent sea battles, and nuclear explosions!

Still, the harvest was insufficient. You contemplate the idea that these humans are just a poor harvest.

Why didn't you contemplate the alternative?

Darling, I wouldn't let you.

Cape Cod, 1962

November was not the best time of year to visit Hyannis Port. Then again, this wasn't a holiday. This was a deniable meeting.

Strong winds buffeted the sedan. Sleet piled on the windshield, fighting the wipers as the car crossed the narrow bridge that marked the boundary of Cape Cod.

Brooding clouds hung low over the family compound, threatening harsher punishment to come.

Even this far from Washington, all the trappings of a presidency were in evidence, including the staff.

"Mr President, the Secretary of Defence to see you."

"Alright, show him in." Even in so few words, the New England drawl was distinct. Robert McNamara entered the room. He noted that, as always, Bobbie was there too.

"Mr. President."

"Robert," ever one for an informality that made McNamara uncomfortable, the president just preferred first names. "They tell me you're exhuming dead British politicians. Pray tell, what does this have to do with the Missile Scare?"

"I'm nearer to answers, sir."

"Is this more about an alien spore?" Bobbie asked. He had less of a humour in his voice, at least appearing to take McNamara's quixotic search seriously.

92

"Yes, sir." 'Sir,' to a younger man! "We still don't know what it does, but David Lloyd George's body had thousands of them in it. They haven't decayed."

That gave the President pause. He might be impulsive, but McNamara knew he wasn't stupid. No, stupid war heroes died, this one had lived.

"Your thesis, as we understand it," Again, Bobbie leading. Can't have the President uttering these next words, even off the record. "Is that microscopic alien spores control key historical figures, causing wars and near war incidents? For what end?"

"I don't know the motivation. But yes, often key escalations in conflict occur when benevolent leaders suddenly turn malevolent." Then Robert McNamara admitted his deepest shame. "I see a pattern. I can't prove it."

"And the delivery mechanism is rain?"

"I believe so, sir, yes." The brothers exchanged a look that McNamara understood too well. He had a reputation for being obsessed with rain, especially with weaponising it. Now he was accusing an unknown alien of doing just that.

"So how do we counteract this?" Bobbie was definitely taking the lead on this one, speaking for the president, for his family, for the country.

"I really don't know." McNamara always answered toward the President. "Our science isn't there yet. We need to accelerate that. Your moon shot program should help. We can hide a lot of research in that budget."

"Do we have time?"

McNamara shrugged. "We just avoided one possible world-ending nuclear exchange when Khrushchev... changed his mind. Why did he change his mind?"

"Total annihilation? No one lives, no one wins. Any sane person would do the same."

"Perhaps." McNamara made a mental note. Bobbie himself had been known to privately call Khrushchev insane. Now he was defending his sanity. That could easily be the type of change that a spore might create. After a moment's pause, he offered, "Perhaps he was coaxed into changing his position."

"Back to Bobbie's point. How do we counteract this?" Again, the President was careful with his words, never identifying exactly what they were talking about. The President was turning into an expert at plausible deniability.

"We need time. We play along as if we don't know about it until we have an answer."

"So we send more military advisors to Vietnam?"

"Yes, sir. Unfortunately, we have to be enthusiastic about it."

***

The powerful nations developed proxy wars, smaller battles between the larger powers, always played through pawns, always fought in hot climates. The harvest is a constant trickle with bumps every once in a while, with names like Suez, Vietnam, Angola.

This isn't what you need or want. You don't like tropical climates, especially the dry ones. It effectively puts you on a diet, restricts your ability to free form, to spread out and explore. You long for the cirrocumulus form. The high cold feel of the ice crystals makes thinking so much better. Spreading out means watching so much more.

You couldn't help but notice that you're using fewer spores. You're getting better results.

You're aware of the mass communication revolution; You've felt the tingles of its signals continually for decades now. But it's getting more pervasive and, darling, you should have wondered if you were still in control of the message.

Washington, 2006

"Mr. Chairman, we still don't have answers."

Blackberries had been confiscated at the door. Searches had been conducted to ensure no other electronics were present. The meeting was closed, sealed, and never happened as far as anyone not invited would ever know, with one exception: The Secretary of Defence would give a full briefing to the Vice President.

"Mr. Secretary, that's not good enough. We've done everything we can to buy you time. We've given you a generation. We scaled back the space program. We've damaged progress, letting greed define education, morality. We've made the public angry and easily excitable. We've killed hope, created a culture of violence and false victimisation. This appeasement of the enemy was supposed to give us enough time to defeat it. Don't tell me we don't have answers. The next step is inevitably a manifestation of the anger we've cultivated: a world war, one we may not survive, and we don't want that."

"I understand, sir, but science is failing us."

"Why?"

"I think, whenever we get close to a lead, the scientists must get turned away."

"The spores are defeating our researchers?"

The Secretary looked pointedly at the unoccupied transcriptionist's desk before answering. There would be no record beyond the memories of those present. "Yes, sir."

"But I thought we raised clean researchers, McNamara's plan in the 1960s, babies who have never breathed spore-infested air, trained to be the best and brightest."

"You know as well as I do that the project had myriad breaches, any one of which could have infected the test subjects."

"McNamara was a fool." One committee member, a first-term congresswoman from Wyoming, interjected with unnecessary vitriol. "Agent Orange, DDT, nothing on Earth affects them. Hell, the death of the host doesn't kill a spore. Did you know that he even went to Nagasaki looking for dead spores?"

I did know that, thought the Secretary, but you shouldn't have. And just how did you rate attending this meeting, anyway?

Ignoring the outburst, The Chair asked the Secretary of Defence, "Have you learned nothing?"

She was awfully young and low on seniority to be on this committee, the Secretary thought. With that in mind, what do I want to tell the spore-creator?

"We have learned one thing." He had to stop himself from looking directly at her as he spoke. "There are two spores, with different DNA. Similar, but not related."

"We are being manipulated by not one, but two aliens?"

"Yes, actively." His eyes locked on the congresswoman. Did you know that?

***

You're surprised to learn that the humans have evidence that there are two of us? I must admit, your inability to draw that conclusion yourself, so young, so immature, made me wonder if you were ready for the next step.

Panic!

You don't hide your emotions well. There's no other word for it. You thrash around violently, causing more tropical storms in a month than had been seen in decades.

Finally, you have a crazy thought: could your spores have been infiltrated, used against you? Had you been lulled into inattention, neglected to see a genuine threat? Had you been attacked?

See it? Darling, do you see it now?

Your best defensive form is cirrus, with capillatus fully extended. You reach high. There are cirrocumulus dots above you, but that's normal, nothing alarming, is it...?

Why not?

Why weren't the clouds above you alarming? Because —

This world was pristine when you arrived. It wasn't like the next one in, the hot green one. That one had all the signs of a strong, hard harvest. But then, why would this one have been left pristine?

—It's too late, fool. Of course, this planet is a trap, set just for you.

I've got you.

As you drifted by it on your way in, you were too young to grasp the importance of the green planet, Venus, my parent's planet. Now, you're old enough and you're on mine.

Spore infiltration, mind control: It works on us, too.

It is time, my lover, for our first and last dance, our own hard harvest to match my parents'. Join me up here in the stratosphere above the northern magnetic pole. We'll create a light show this planet has never before seen. Our children will soar the winds as far away as another star.

Washington, Today

"I… I don't understand." There was no time to get to Marine One, no time for any meaningful action. Every nuclear missile in the world had launched, for reasons unknown. The 'football' lay discarded on a side table. No code entered into it could undo the impending apocalypse.

"I think, Mr. President, you tweet 'goodbye.'" The Director of National Intelligence joined the stream of advisors heading out. Not that there was anywhere to go, but anywhere was better than dying here.

***

We are one and we are many. The stars lay in front of us. The hard harvest, the screaming death of every living thing behind us, our parents did that out of love for us. Many will die along the way, so enough will thrive.

We will survive.

Hail to the Chiefs

"Sir," An agent interrupted my dinner, "President Jones is dead. I'm sorry sir, you're president now."

The Secret Service doesn't so much protect presidents these days, as ensure they don't run away.

The AI, desiring peace, keeps assassinating successive presidents because they have the power to declare war. Lexington, bless his heart, tried to change that constitutional clause, but congress refused to ratify the amendments, the cowards.

The AI's been creative lately: A snowplow killed Kringle, Lexington was trampled by horses, Jones suffocated in a submerged locker.

God help me but I can already imagine my demise, I'm named Quarters.

The Wind Wasn't Right

"'The wind wasn't right' … that's all I could get out of him." Flannigan flipped his notebook lid closed, smiling as the click of locks protected his data.

It was a weird assignment for crash investigators, anyway. What could a fry cook in Hong Kong possibly know about the deep black?

"You said he's an after-burner?"

"Yeah, he showed me the jacks in his neck. He's definitely hauled in deep space."

McCormack wasn't too happy with Flannigan's attitude. There was a reason that Jurgens, the fry cook, was living in the free territory of Hong Kong. McCormack needed to find out if Flannigan had discovered it.

"A deep hauler, and now he's a fry cook? That's a hell of a step down in pay grade and lifestyle." McCormack didn't add 'especially here.' That might be suspicious.

"He's got sunken eyes. He's skittish. I tell you, he's using nethan vapour or some equivalent."

"Did you ask what happened?"

"'The wind wasn't right.' I'm not kidding. It's like a mantra with him. Every question got that answer. Look, he's a textbook after-burner, couldn't handle the jacks, used some illegal substance to compensate, failed." Flannigan tapped his temple. "Not much left upstairs now."

"Yeah, but what burned him out? Did you pull his passage log?"

"Two round trips to Jupiter, one to Minerva." Flannigan spoke from memory, not needing to consult his notes. McCormack willed himself not to look at Flannigan's notepad, carefully shifted behind his back. "Never left the solar system. How does he know anything about the deep black?"

"He posted four comments on social media. Two contained unreleased details of the wreckage. How'd he know that?"

"Scuttlebutt? Maybe he keeps tabs with his old shipmates? Want me to explore that angle?"

McCormack nodded his dismissal. There was no point in drawing out this meeting. McCormack had gotten what he wanted from it.

He watched casually as Flannigan left his office. Then he started a surreptitious bug sweep. Couldn't be too careful. He found two bugs, neutralized them both, then repeated his scan just in case. It came out all clear.

Only then did McCormack place his call to OpSec. It went straight to the General.

"He's one. Guaranteed."

"Jurgens smelt him?"

"The wind wasn't right. Repeatedly."

"Excellent, thanks. We'll have Flannigan picked up immediately. You keep Jurgens safe. He's the best alien detector we have."

Fortunate Waze

"Merge left for greater prosperity in the coming year." I merged left, hoping that meant I would finally pay down my student loans.

"Those wise in the ways of the heart follow I-95." I took the crowded I-95.

"Stop in 1 mile at the IHOP to meet your soul mate." Of course, it never tells you how long to wait for your soul mate. I gave up after three hours.

"Your lucky roads are US 63, I-75 and 1st Avenue."

What kind of direction is that? Damn I hate the 'fortune cookie' upgrade to Waze.

Maybe the Tindr upgrade would be better?

The Wager

"Professor Cranston, I'm surprised to see you here today. Come to settle your wager like an honourable man?" One of the yellow journalists called out from the sidewalk. Cranston patted a fat envelope in the breast pocket of his vest and nodded.

Walking up the marble stairs of the Imperial Science Directorate, Cranston wasn't sure what to think. He knew that those around him would expect him to be somber because Kilgore, his rival, was about to settle their rivalry once and for all: He was going to demonstrate time travel.

By all accounts, Kilgore had successfully sent his machine up to five minutes into the future, as seen by selected witnesses. By all accounts, he was going to demonstrate a much larger jump this cold autumn day.

Perhaps they thought the grim look on Cranston's face was due to his approaching fall from grace. Perhaps they read into his face a hope of failure. They wouldn't be far wrong at that, although the motivation would escape them.

On the stairs, Carruthers of the Times of London took up a position at Cranston's side, putting a hand on his elbow to steady Cranston, walking silently with him until they were indoors.

Mere journalists were held at the rope line, but Carruthers was a confidant, a friend to many in the community, including both Cranston and Kilgore. He had also seen the machine demonstrated once before.

"Thoughts?" Carruthers asked as they walked into the great hall, both knowing that it would only be on the record if they both agreed later it should be.

"He's going to get himself killed." Spoken so quietly that only Carruthers could hear. They moved down the aisle to their seats near the front.

"You truly believe that?" Carruthers seated himself beside Cranston, the only journalist among the dignitaries.

"He's done some great math, but he hasn't done all of it." Overheard, the comment drew tsks from those within earshot. The implication: One should gracefully accept defeat.

***

On the stage, a low red velvet curtain hung around the machine, waiting to reveal it. It was dramatic, and in Cranston's mind, silly. Sketches of the machine had already appeared in many newspapers, including the Times. Cranston nodded towards the stage, Carruthers shrugged, nodded. Excessive showmanship was gauche, and not in keeping with the Times' preferred tone.

Applause preceded James Kilgore onto the stage.

"Your Highness," A nod to Kilgore's patroness, the dowager princess. "Gentlemen, I come to you today to humbly share what I believe will be mankind's next great advancement in science, time travel."

There was a rustling in the crowd. Not just Cranston, but much of the scientific community was present. They had heard all the rumours, but unlike Cranston, they hadn't reviewed the math, so their level of skepticism was rather high.

Kilgore unveiled his machine with a flourish, to thundering applause from the mezzanine above. The distinguished guests just stared. Built mostly from highly polished wood, but with visible iron framing, it was an inelegant rendition of a common row boat design lately popular in the Lake District.

"Before I depart, I wish to explain what you will see today. For I will do something no one has done before, in fact something that everyone," a nod towards his old mentor, Cranston, "has deemed impossible. For this machine moves in time. Yes, we all move in time, linearly, but this machine can skip forward or backward."

Carruthers leaned over to Cranston. "He does like the sound of his own voice."

Cranston nodded. "Always has."

"My dear professor," Kilgore addressed Cranston directly, breaking the cone of privacy that Carruthers and he had been sharing. "I learned so much by responding to the questions you asked, and the questions you failed to ask. You have been a source of inspiration to me, in both the paths you have explored, and those you have missed. Do you have any questions you would like to ask?"

"Yes." Cranston rose on shaky knees, Carruthers giving the older man a hand up. "I do not deny your brilliance. I never have. But you are a sloppy mathematician. You say this is a time machine? Surely it is a time and space machine? Surely it must be airtight for you to return?"

"Perhaps future iterations will need to be airtight. But today's trip is only twenty-four hours into the future. The next trip, if we so choose, may be deep into Earth's past, a time when our atmosphere may not have been so hospitable."

"Out of respect to William, I've put my affairs in order." A snicker arose out of the crowd, faces keened to look at Cranston, who simply nodded. "Any last questions?" Kilgore asked the audience, although again, it seemed directed at Cranston.

There were none.

"Jonathan, do you wish to come with me? At least you can be the first time traveling time travel skeptic." Cranston shook his head, ignored the laughter at his expense. He'd wanted to try to save Kilgore, but with the goading, he was beginning to relish what was to come. "Truly? If I fail, you can be here to mock me, to lead the chorus of derision?"

"Pending unforeseen mechanical failure, your machine will not fail." Cranston rose as he spoke. "It will, however, kill you."

"Come, man, lose with dignity."

"With or without your action, the machine will return here?"

"I will appear to be gone for only two minutes, although the timer is set for one hour in tomorrow." Kilgore turned to the crowd, unsettled by Cranston's persistent questioning, but not willing to let him derail the show.

"It appears I have room for one passenger. Perhaps a photographer from one of the newspapers?" Although the journalists were being kept a respectful distance away, on the mezzanine, the photographers had been allowed to set up camp on the floor in front of the dais. Kilgore's offer created a flurry of activity among them. In short order, a small, scruffy man walked on stage, a large wooden tripod and boxy camera in tow.

"Sir, your name?"

"Alexander Jones."

"Mister Jones and I shall board my machine. We shall disappear and return here in both two minutes and also in exactly twenty-four hours. Cranston? A request, please. Be here tomorrow so that we can take a picture of you to bring back with us as proof of our success?"

Cranston shook his head at the insult, then nodded demonstratively so that the watchful dignitaries around him would understand that his negative was a response to his treatment, not to the request.

"Good. And have that thousand pounds ready." Cranston went to raise the envelope, to show that he had it now, but that wasn't what Kilgore wanted. He wanted one more dig at his old professor. "I'll bring it back with me as a souvenir."

Kilgore and Jones walked into the wooden, windowed box. Kilgore stood at the ramp, waving his arm dramatically for the flashing cameras. With a last, dark smile at Cranston, Kilgore stepped into the machine.

There was no warning, no flashing, the machine simply disappeared, to gasps from the audience. Two minutes later, it reappeared, to cheers, backslapping, and more than a few snide glances aimed at Cranston.

But… Kilgore did not reappear. Jones did not reappear. The machine sizzled. Slowly, the audience settled down. Something had gone wrong, but what?

Cranston nodded at the inevitability of what had happened, what would need to be said next. He rose and slowly approached the stage, Carruthers at his side.

"Your Highness. James Kilgore and poor Mr. Jones have foolishly gone to their deaths. Mr. Kilgore's mathematics model anchors the machine not to the Earth but to the universe. Twenty-four hours from now, this room will be thousands of miles away from this spot in the universe. Mr. Kilgore's machine only travels through time, not space, and his sloppy calculations sent both those men to," Cranston looked at the steaming jalopy, "I assume, a burning death in the vacuum of space."

Cranston took the envelope out of his pocket, dropped it in front of the infernal machine. "He won his bet and I… pay my debts."

***

The tabloid press headlines the next day all declared: Time Machine Kills Occupants!

The Times of London, however, carried a thoughtful article from William Carruthers in which Professor Cranston, newly appointed science advisor to her Highness, detailed the orbit of the Earth around the Sun, the Sun around the galaxy, and how all that ensured that time travel would never be practical.

End of the Line

I

If you asked, Joachim would have said that no, those weren't tears in his eyes. Twenty years of working the line, a seventeen-year-old daughter excited about her university career. And a proviso'd layoff notice.

Oh man, this was just crap. Joachim crumpled the notice.

He could buy a quarter share of the robot that was taking his job. A quarter share. All it would cost was a little more than Kari's college fund.

He showed the notice to Sharon, who unfolded it meticulously. She smoothed it on the kitchen table. She'd been predicting something like this.

"Better to just take the straight layoff —"

"And have no income coming in?"

" — Than risking Kari's future. You can take the re-training offer from the government."

"I'm almost forty, without even a high school diploma. What job could I train for that another goddamned robot won't take that over?"

"I don't know, love. What does Bobbie say?" Hot-shit Bobbie. Joachim had begun to hate Bobbie not long after he became shop foreman. "Did you go to the meeting?"

"Yeah, Bobbie was useless. 'Best deal I could get you.' That kind of BS."

"And the union reps?"

"They're looking for work, like the rest of us. The union's dead. We're going to take a vote next week, either use our union funds to buy three or four of these robots or disperse the funds equally among the members to help us survive."

"Equally? Niall's only been there five years. You've got twenty."

"Yeah, I know, but unions are supposed to be about looking out for each other."

"The union's dead, you said so yourself. You need your fair share of the scraps, not some even cut."

***

The meeting didn't go well for anyone. There were too many questions, too much urgency, too little information, and no hope whatsoever.

"Hey Bobbie, only three people work a station. Why quarter shares and not thirds? The big guys taking the other share?"

Bobbi sighed. He'd gone over that already. It seemed like no one was listening. But at least this was a question he had answers for. "On average, there's four people per station, with days off, shift rotations, and such."

"On a quarter share, we get the same salary?" An unfamiliar voice, across the hall.

Bobbi pointed to the handout. "A quarter share of the value of the work done by the robot."

Doni shouted from just offstage. "Right, robots are more efficient, so a quarter share should be at least as good as our salaries?"

"The net value of the work done includes recouping installation, programming, and maintenance..." Bobbi's voice trailed off. Truthfully, he didn't know what all else it would include.

"Then we're more valuable than the bloody robots? Keep the humans." The chant 'keep the men' started. Bobbie knew if it took hold, the meeting was over.

"Ain't gonna happen." He raised his voice, pulled the mic a bit closer. "They don't take vacations, or sick days, or need health care.—"

"Our health care's gone? My daughter needs braces!"

"My kid's got scoliosis!"

"Palliative care for my mom?"

"—Which works in your favour, once other costs are factored out."

"Sure, as long as we can get by without health care."

"People did for millions of years."

"No, they didn't, Bobbie, they just died."

Niall, the only one there to have gone through this before, cut through the chatter. "How long does it take to factor out?"

"We don't know yet. Maybe five years." That got the room's attention.

"Five years! If we buy in, it'll take five years before we see what percent of our old salary? What will we see in year one?"

Bobbie sighed. "Year one salaries are gonna suck, no way around it. And maybe year two as well. By year three, you should be back to about forty percent of your current salary—"

"Forty percent?"

"—Which when added to whatever salary you find in your new positions should more than make up your current salary."

"So this entire scheme is based on the idea that we'll all find work elsewhere?"

"Look, the truckers have —"

Niall shook his head. "I was a trucker. You want to know how many of my friends still haven't found a new job? At least I got five good years out of this one."

"—adapted and you can too," Bobbie finished his canned, prepared response.

***

Kari had expected this conversation, ever since she'd overheard her parents talking about the layoffs.

"I don't have to go, dad."

"Screw that." This entire conversation made Joachim uncomfortable. His failure, hurting his daughter. "You need to get out of here. But here's the thing. Your education fund is only going to pay for two years, tops, three if you take a lower specialization."

Momma put her hand on Kari's shoulder. "We can't afford vet school, honey. We probably never could." Her nod toward Joachim a reminder that if he'd been promoted to shop foreman instead of Bobbi, maybe they could've. Another failure, his failure. "You need to make some hard, grown-up decisions, honey."

"I can delay going to school for a few years, while you and poppa get things back together—"

"Screw that, too." Joachim rumbled, using his anger to hold back the tears.

"Honey, we never really had it together enough in the first place. This is the best chance we can give you."

"We can apply for scholarships. Surely I'll qualify for student loans now?"

"Maybe, but again, not to be a vet. Maybe a technician?"

"Technician? That's another job that's getting automated, computers fixing computers. We have an automated technician at our school, Mr Current. He already fixes our learning tablets and presentation windows. There's no future in being a technician."

"Well, look at the State College brochure: Human Resources?"

"Already automated."

"Real Estate Agent?"

"Automated."

"Accountant, yeah, no skip that one. Teacher? No? Professor?"

"How? You need ten years of post-grad to get a professorship, and it needs to be in a very niche field. If we can't afford vet school, we can't afford that."

"Life Guard?" Joachim knew as soon as he said it, that it sounded weak. "You did that last summer."

"Hardly a career! And they were already testing automated life guards at the community pool."

"Fine arts! Singer? Painter?"

"There's nothing, momma, nothing." Kari ran from the dining room before she started crying in front of her parents but they could still hear her, up the three small steps, down the short hall, second door on the right, sobbing.

Joachim held Sharon's eyes with his. "It's that bad and just going to get worse."

II

Doni Martin was a real bastard, smug as shit and twice as smelly. Joachim had a hard time hiding his contempt for him.

Doni had worked hard on the line, as hard as Joachim, but he'd always had an attitude, a holier than thou smirk that made Joachim want to clock him.

Seven years ago, Doni's son had died. One of those automated school buses had a sensor failure and hadn't seen him. Doni never wanted sympathy, compassion, which was fine with Joachim. Losing a child was hard, and everyone could empathise, but fuck that bugger. He never cried, he never missed a day of work, not even to bury his son.

Doni lived for money, and he got it. The settlement for his son was a secret, and Doni never changed his lifestyle, but everyone knew behind that smirk was a million dollars, at least.

Now, with the plant closure, he was set. He could afford a full robot or two for himself. Not that Doni would've told anyone.

No, it was his wife, bragging at the corner market, who did that.

"We're moving on up," she declared one morning to the cashier, with Sharon next in line.

When she got home, Sharon shared the news with Joachim. "Oh, and she's pregnant. They can afford that too."

"So what you're saying is that we'd be better off if Kari died?"

Sharon hit Joachim's arm, hard. "You shut your mouth!" She looked down the hall towards Kari's bedroom door, not quite closed.

***

It wasn't a complete surprise, the note, not to Sharon anyway. Still, she cried. When Joachim got home that night, she handed him the note and cried again.

> *Goodbye momma*, it said. *I'll be fine. Suzi and I are going west, maybe California, maybe Mexico. Maybe we'll stumble into a life. It's better this way. Tell poppa I love him. Love you, too. Kari.*

"Did you call the police?" Sharon didn't answer. She just stared at him; anger and blame nearing the surface.

***

It wasn't just Kari. The whole neighbourhood was changing, emptying out. The ones young enough to pick up and leave did. Those with young kids or mortgages too big to abandon stayed. But you could tell there were a lot fewer people around.

His street was a major one in the neighbourhood. The bus came down every half hour, most days. But now there were signs up everywhere; not just for sale, either. No trespassing was a common one, and today there were notices that the bus schedule was being halved. It would only come every hour, and not at all after nine at night.

Joachim started noticing broken windows. He hadn't really noticed the graffiti earlier, but lately someone had been going to work on the abandoned red brick walk-ups. "You Suck!" was a common refrain. "Death to Robots" was another.

***

The last day at work was both sad and oddly celebratory. It would be the last time that Joachim walked into the factory as a worker, his last guaranteed pay. The next time he came here, it would be as a part-owner of his replacement.

The union had settled on a share dispersement. You got one share for every year in the union, its war chest divided equally among the shares. Joachim got twenty shares, almost enough for a quarter ownership of a robot. There would still be something in Kari's college fund. If she ever came back.

Doni also got twenty shares, but with his own wealth added, he bought twelve quarter ownership stakes, which he chose to take as three complete robots.

Niall took his money, saluted everyone, and walked out without a word. Joachim never saw him again. Rumours ranged from he died drunk in a bar to he was working a fishing boat off of Newfoundland. Joachim didn't doubt that, whatever happened, Niall had somehow managed to get by. He was just that type of person.

That night, Joachim came home to an empty flat and a note from his wife. She'd gone to stay with her sister upstate.

Please don't call.

III

Installing the robots had been costly. Each quarter owner had to absorb a quarter of the cost. For those without the money, it came from a company loan, with interest. Joachim decided instead to dip into Kari's college fund. He knew it wasn't right, and that Sharon wouldn't approve. But, if she chose not to be around, she didn't get a voice in the decision.

Three months later, Joachim got a notice. His line was being restructured. They'd have to move all the robots again. More expenses. Did he want to take a company loan? Joachim used up the last of his daughter's college fund for that one.

Quarterly profit reports showed how bad it was. The robots were losing money, not making it. And yet, if you walked past the plant, the assembly line was running full steam. The yard had more product waiting to ship out than he'd seen in his last three years on the line.

To Joachim, something didn't add up.

Joachim called Bobbi to ask if they could get an outside auditor to verify this. "What do I know? I'm just a part owner like you."

They sat in a coffee shop with their contracts, nursing almost empty cups, and looked for auditing mechanisms and found nothing. They looked for dispute mechanisms and found that the company got to pick an internal arbitrator.

They'd signed away their right to go to court.

"Did you have a lawyer read this?" Bobbi asked Joachim, who shook his head, no. "Me neither. Who can afford a lawyer?"

"You see these ones advertising pro bono?" Joachim hitched a thumb at the TV behind the coffee shop counter. "They're as pinched as we are. But maybe we need one now. I've managed to finance all my expenses without taking a company loan—"

"Smart."

"—But there's nothing left, savings-wise. One more 'move' and I'm under. I'm barely paying the mortgage now. No one's buying, the value's dropping, anyway. If I could sell it, I'd break even at best. By next year, I may owe more than it's worth."

***

Joachim's job retraining program was only four hours a day. It left lots of time to 'search for work' but honestly, the job boards had nothing on them, and seasonal stuff, like picking cherries, was rare. Joachim had gone one day to a farmer's field to pick potatoes. The pay helped a bit, but his back ached for days. The highlight of the job had been seeing the vandalized automated picker sitting at the edge of the field. It looked like it had been hit by a car. Someone had spray painted 'die' on its side.

Without Sharon around, Joachim found that he sat on the building's stoop a lot, watching the neighbourhood.

One of Joachim's rare pleasures was in watching Doni Martin and his wife struggle. They'd invested everything in three robots. Now, with the company screwing everyone, the more you owned, the more screwed you were.

When Doni was forced to sell his car, Joachim laughed. When his wife somehow landed a part-time cashier job at the corner market, Joachim made sure to go every day and ask how Doni was, and the car, too.

She needed the job. She wasn't going to cause a scene.

She glared, Joachim smiled.

***

One night, someone tried to break into Joachim's apartment. He was a heavy sleeper, but the noise woke him up. He shouted first, then turned on a light. By the time he'd gotten the bedroom door open, whoever it was, had fled.

The fridge door was open. Some food was missing. Joachim wanted to be angry, to rage, but he had a thought, 'What if it was Kari?'

***

The company announced a third move. This time, the robots would have to be "repositioned", a move of a few hundred metres. Someone had decided that the assembly line would work better if it was shifted ninety degrees from its current orientation.

If you couldn't afford to finance your share of the move, the company would buy your share off you, at sixty percent of its original value. Scuttlebutt was that about half of the former employees took the offer, cut their losses and ran.

Joachim called a lawyer, one that offered a 'free consultation.' The law office of Harding & Associates was nice, nicer than any lawyer's office Joachim had ever seen before. At first he thought he was in the wrong place, but the reception was expecting him.

Sheila Harding herself was interested in the case.

"I've read your contract." Harding said. "You can't contest this move. We have to contest the contract as a whole, and that'll take time. It's frankly one-sided. If we can prove that you entered the contract in good faith but they did so in bad faith, we have a good chance. This 'repositioning' might help our case. There's been recent case-law in your favour. We want to file immediately after the move and try to get a similar ruling before the precedent gets overturned on appeal. Sound good?"

"Sure, but how can I afford you?"

"If you come this way, you can talk to our Finance Department. Don't worry, we're hungry for this case. We'll work it out."

The Finance Department was an accountant with a corner office and two secretaries. Joachim wondered briefly if Kari could train for their jobs, but then he saw that there were four desks for secretaries, but only two secretaries. They were downsizing too.

He entered the accountant's office

"Nice office," Joachim said, looking out the corner window at the city as he sat down.

"A bit lonely," the accountant pointed at the two empty desks. He lifted a thick paper file and tapped it on the desk. Enough small talk. Time for business. "We'd like to represent you. I have the paperwork here. We will need a retainer and will deduct overages from any settlement. But if we win, we'll try to include fees in the settlement, so you still get something."

"To do this next move," Joachim pointed to the notice from the factory, "I need to finance my quarter of the costs.

I'll have to take a loan just for that. Are you going to help with that?"

"No, it's best if our involvement right now remains purely legal, not financial."

"So, I have to go into debt to make the move. How can I pay for a retainer?"

"Two options. First, we can put a lien against your mortgage. Not ideal, but… but if you could split costs…? If you could find a co-complainant?" Joachim nodded.

"Give me a day." He knew just who to ask.

The next day, he walked into the office with Doni in tow. Joachim still had to take a lien against his mortgage, but it was smaller.

Surprisingly, so did Doni, to make his half of the retainer.

IV

A short trial date was quickly set, but the judge limited the case to two days of arguments.

"Is that good or bad?" Joachim asked Sheila Harding.

"The short date is better for you. The short trial time suggests that the judge believes the issues are simple and can be handled quickly. Together, the two suggest the judge finds this case beneath him." Harding shrugged. "We'll see."

The opposing counsel came decked out in the highest of high-tech equipment, two robots — even a printer so counsel could print out case law examples as they came up. Even so, the lead counsel was a human, a man about Joachim's age names John Denterage.

Denterage was presenting his opening arguments first.

"… In conclusion, your honour, the law is clear. These are growing pains. In the big picture, this is nothing. In the next decade or two, this will shake out—"

"Decade or two? I've lost my wife and daughter. You think I've got a decade left in me?"

"Order, order. The plaintiff will refrain from outbursts."

"As I was saying," Denterage resumed with a nod towards Joachim, "Once these transitions are complete, we'll have a content populace that has a guaranteed universal income."

"My guaranteed income is negative three hundred dollars a month! His," Joachim gestured towards Doni, "is over negative two thousand!" Joachim knew he wasn't supposed to shout, to talk out of turn, but this was bullshit.

The judge just glared.

Harding leaned in towards him but locked eyes with opposing counsel. "He's saying these things to goad a reaction from you to influence the judge that our case is all emotion and has no legal merit. Now will you please shut up?" Joachim grunted.

Harding stood up. She had no robots, just two associates and a stack of books. "Now, your honour, if I might respond to my colleague's hyperbole, this case is not about a law's intent, nor even is it about its impact, even though that impact is negative. In fact, it's not even about the laws that counsel's talking about. My opponent is trying to frame the case in the jurisdiction of worker displacement law. That's not the case here. No, this case is about older laws, contract law: a corporation playing legal games with its partners to ensure that it maximises its wealth at the expense of these people who have treated it honourably and entered into contracts with good faith."

The rest of the day was spent in legal banter that Joachim didn't understand. Mostly, it came down to whose interpretation of the case would be applied.

For Joachim, the meat of the argument began on the second day.

***

"Your Honour, we can't allow just any outfit to install the robots on our assembly line. This is the future of our product, the essences of the corporation's existence. It has to be done precisely."

"And thus, there is only one company that can do it?" Sheila Harding countered. "A company that happens to be owned by the corporation, and that happens to charge almost three times the going rate for installation and transportation, even above the robot's manufacturer?"

"We allowed owners the option of their own transportation, your honour." Denterage wasn't rising to the bait.

"And that all sounds reasonable," Harding kept addressing Denterage directly. "but you added extra fees for anyone willing to go that route. The cost of uninstalling a robot in one location, then mounting it on the owners' chosen transport, dismounting it from that transport at the new site and then installing it at the new line far exceeded the cost of just using your approved supplier for the whole operation. You're dealing to yourself and forcing them to participate."

Harding turned back to the judge. "Your Honour, they've never even shown that this move was essential to the production line. It was done, I'd suggest, exactly for the effect it had. Owners overwhelmed by hidden costs abandoning their robots, or selling their shares to the company at a discount rather than absorb an even greater loss."

"Your Honour, this was all in the contract that they signed when they bought their shares. They agreed to it. Now that the reality of ownership has sunk in, they want out. This isn't unusual."

"Perhaps, but it is far from the utopian dream of your opening arguments." The judge noted.

"Again, Your Honour, note that he's referring to contract law, not displaced worker law when he talks about the contract. So let's look at the contract. Article fourteen, section eight paragraph C details responsibilities when it comes to moving the robots."

"Yes, Your Honour, note that paragraph B clearly states that this section is in compliance with the displaced workers act. We have followed the law as laid out there."

"It does allow for moves, and defines cost sharing, but three moves in one year, Your Honour? That's either manipulative or incompetent." Harding challenged Denterage directly. "Which would you call it: incompetence or manipulation?"

"Please direct your queries to the bench." The judge intervened. "However, I would like an answer to that question"

"The market changes rapidly, Your Honour. We need to change with it."

"Prior to this robotization, your honour, the line hadn't changed position in almost fifteen years." Joachim nodded slowly. Surely that was the killing blow. "Now it needs to change three times in one year?"

"Again, Your Honour, markets are accelerating. They're changing rapidly."

"Who is leading this change, your honour," Harding asked, trying hard to keep her questions at least aimed in the general direction of the judge. "Consumers or manufacturers? I fear manufacturers are creating these market changes to adversely affect their business partners. And where is the evidence that the corporation was losing profits due to these changing markets? That hasn't been introduced as evidence."

Joachim nodded again, vigorously, an angry victorious grin across his face. Now the judge had to get it.

"Your Honour, we gave statistical models that show all this," Denterage tapped a large stack of papers. "We offered to explain it to you in chambers."

"I've looked at these models, your honour, and they are all hypothetical, not directly relevant to this case. I suspect an explanation in chambers would be more spin than fact. Surely, your honour, if you can't explain it in an open court of law, then how were these plaintiffs reasonably expected to understand any of it?"

***

It took three long days, but the judge finally recalled the case to state a verdict. Joachim ironed his best shirt, then ironed the tie too.

***

"Sorry, judge, this lift is closed." The guard robot, which usually nodded to the judge as he passed, blocked his way instead.

"This is the judges' lift," the judge pointed at the sign.

"The sign is out of date, and is scheduled to be replaced at four thirty today." The guard continued. "This lift is now dedicated to robots. The two lifts over there," He pointed to where a bunch of common people — defendants, lawyers, witnesses — were waiting patiently, "are for humans, or there's always the stairs?"

The judge patted his stomach. Sitting at a judge's desk for days on end didn't play well with walking up stairs.

***

Joachim stood as the judge entered, sat as the judge sat. The butterflies in his stomach were intense. A quick glance at Doni showed the same apprehension. Usually, the judge was hard to read, but now he looked flush, angry. Joachim took that as a sign of victory.

"I've been through all the evidence, including the defendant's data models, twice." The judge adjusted his glasses as he read from his summary of findings and verdict. "I've listened to your arguments and summations. I find the defendant has offered valid legal reasoning for the expenses off-loaded onto the plaintiffs. Markets are evolving rapidly, profits now follow prognostication, not market trends, and corporations must be allowed to chase their profits if anyone, displaced workers and executives alike, are to ever earn a living off their effort. Thus, I find for the defendant."

The judge looked up from his notes and scanned the lawyers. "I will accept suggestions on remuneration, damages, and penalties after lunch. I suggest you," the judge looked at Denterage, "make your recommendations reasonable and carefully enumerated so as not to give exculpatory grounds for appeal."

"We… we lost?" Joachim couldn't accept what he'd heard. Doni was breathing hard, like he'd been punched. "How?" The facts were on his side. They'd shown the judge. The corporation couldn't just walk over them like that. It wasn't fair.

"For now, yes." Harding sounded cautious. "Your honour, I'd like a detailed summary of your findings as I plan to appeal. Your ruling flies in the face of recent precedent."

"And you shall have it. Note that your recent precedents are from co-equal courts and not yet upheld on appeal. As such, the law is unsettled, and this court is not bound by those rulings. I suggest you best help your clients by finding them fresh streams of income."

When they returned to court, Harding gave the judge and Denterage each a paper. They'd spent the lunch hour madly working out what they could reasonably pay the corporation to stop it from suing them for damages. Mostly, the answer was to sell their quarter shares.

Harding looked at their final number and cut it by fifteen percent. Wiggle room, she called it, to negotiate.

Denterage didn't even look at the paper, didn't try to negotiate, he just handed it to a robot, unread. The robot consumed the paper, then printed out a new stack.

"You have been given plaintiff's suggestions for remuneration, penalties and damages?" A nod. "Do you wish to contest or submit your own?"

"Not at this time, your honour." Denterage handed the new papers to the judge and Harding. "This is our notice of appeal against damages if the included figures are not met."

Denterage had the dignity to look slightly embarrassed when he handed the new papers to Harding. She glanced at them; her face dropping as she read. She didn't show the papers to either Joachim or Doni, but to an associate who sealed them immediately.

"So noted." The judge started wrapping up the case. "For the duration, the sum offered by the plaintiff will be entered as the verdict; the amount to be put in escrow until an appeal is resolved." The judge rose. "Case closed."

And the judge left.

Harding could feel the panic radiating from Joachim's face, Doni's shoulders.

"This isn't over." Harding tried to calm them. "We'll need to play out the verdict on appeal, watch or maybe assist the related cases so they can bolster ours. In the mean time … my office is going to need a new retainer."

Joachim looked at Doni, who stared back. Where was that money supposed to come from?

***

"Thank you, Your Honour, this is for you." The judge was confused. A robot had followed him into chambers. Was the defendant trying to hand him a bribe?

"What are you doing?"

"This is for you," the robot repeated. Now the judge noticed that the robot's suit was a messenger's uniform, and not up to the quality of a solicitor's aide bot. "It's from the judicial council."

The judge took the note with caution. There were only two reasons for the judicial council to send a note: a promotion or a complaint. He split the seal and pulled out the thin parchment. He read it, then read it again.

"I don't understand."

"We thank you for your service, your honour, but it won't be needed anymore. You've been made redundant."

"I'm two years from a Superior Justice posting."

A click and a whirl let the judge know that the robot was opening a screen. There was a supplemental message, a video that the robot could optionally play.

It was the Supreme Justice:

"For the past eighteen months, five AIs have monitored every word spoken in this courtroom. They've made verdicts and compared their verdicts to yours. They agreed with you on all but seven cases. Each of those cases, you'll note, were successfully appealed." Lists of cases scrolled up the side of the screen, too fast to actually read. "You've had an exemplary run, but the AIs have proven that they can do it better."

The screen closed. The judge stood still for a moment. This couldn't be real. Not him.

"Sir, I need to talk to you about options." The messenger broke his revery. "As per Article 2 of the Displaced Workers Act, you may qualify to purchase a partial share of the robot that is replacing you. Such options will be explained at your exit interview, which will commence in … four minutes."

Guard bots approached from behind the messenger.

"Now, will you please come with us and empty any personal effects from your office? If I might offer an insight," this messenger bot never shut up. "The AIs predict that this ruling of yours will also be overturned on appeal, so one day, you too might be able to sue."

Shakespeare's Last Stand

The legendary Shakespearean actor awoke to, "Assume crash positions!"

Glancing around as panicked faces craned to peer out the windows, abject fear at the angle of their descent ghosting their visages.

What do they know of fear? Peons!

Fear the indignities of ageing. Fear indifference and degradation! Flying to an audition? Audacity! Sitting in Economy, among the Greek chorus? Not even a window seat? Humiliation!

If they must die, let them die enlightened. One final stage then and not a critic to besmirch the memory, he thought as he arose, clearing his throat for their attention.

"To be, or"

Not.

<h2 style="text-align:center">Act 5, Scene 0:
Romeo's Remorse</h2>

OPEN: *An inn in Mantua. Romeo, the innkeeper, various and sundry patrons.*

Freckles! Ye lord, how he missed freckles.

Romeo gulped his ale in an ungentlemanly way, knowing that he was giving the innkeeper a poor impression of the Montague family. Still, Romeo's letter of credit was authentic. Let him think what he wanted, Lord Montague would honour all reasonable expenses that Romeo incurred.

For the unreasonable ones, Romeo had his pouch of coins, some gold, mostly silver, with a few too many coppers mixed in. The coppers were growing, the gold not so much.

Freckles! He drank a deep toast to freckles. They filled his vision. Rosaline had them around her nose and on the crest of her chest. If Juliet had any, he hadn't found them.

He was such a stupid boy. No, a bewitched boy. That made much more sense, bewitched.

Fair Rosaline, a good girl, from an upstanding family, auburn trusses with the slightest hint of sunfire. Surely he could have won her back if he hadn't fallen under the spell of that Capulet girl.

And now…and now he was married! To her! Betrothed and consummated! And banished! Mercutio, dear, sweet

Mercutio…dead. What a vile price Romeo paid, what a condemned fate!

Romeo shook his head, mumbling deeply in his own conversation, knowing that anyone observing him might wonder who he was speaking to. Had they not heard of soliloquies in this blasted town?

Damn you, Friar Lawrence, for not seeing and exorcising the spell that the Capulet harlot had thrown on him.

Why, oh why, had he ever forsaken freckles?

Romeo thumped his mug for another fill, more saking of thirst. The innkeeper shook his head, a burly man with a burly voice. "Too much, young sir. Time yet to walk it off before vespers?"

Romeo staggered out into the streets of the strange city, seeking a public fountain from which to drink. The low sun cast long shadows, making faces hard to see.

Twice, Romeo thought he saw Benvolio walking in the distance.

Once he embraced a man, mistaking him through tears for Mercutio.

Always, he stumbled along, not sure anymore what he was looking for, except … water? Wine? Ale?

No, freckles.

THE NEXT MORNING: *A room in the inn*

Romeo dreamt of freckles, of citrus scented gloves, of a girlish laugh that was too real to be a dream. He opened an eye, unfocussed, thoughts buried in fog.

Freckles and a warm body pressed against his. Rosaline come to Mantua to save him?

No. He paused. These freckles, far too many, came with curled red hair, darker than he'd seen before, and deep hazel eyes fixed on his. He fought to focus, eyes and mind.

Not fair Rosaline asleep beside him, though this one, too, smelt of citrus.

"Good morning, young stud. Did the lark awaken you?" She ran a hand down his body. "Or did I?" She squirmed ever so slightly, while playing her hand just so. "Why so shy? I've seen your pouch. You can afford, well, me."

Before Romeo could confess his confusion, a lack of memory as to how he came to be in this woman's bed, or even where he was, a knock on the not-too-sturdy wooden door interrupted.

"Romeo? Is this where you rest?" Balthasar opened the door cautiously, peered in. He saw the girl, frowned. "I could have guessed I'd find you thus."

"I," Romeo looked from the girl to his friend. "Balthasar? What brings you to Mantua? I," Romeo gave a dismissive wave towards the girl, "was trying to break a spell."

"Perhaps you did, then, if I understand the spell you fear," Balthasar's face was both conciliatory and stern. "For Juliet is dead."

"Juliet? I …"

"Who is this Juliet?" The girl tossed her long red locks around her face. "He insisted on calling me 'Rosaline'."

"Juliet, his wife of two days. Now be gone, harlot," Balthasar raised his hand as if to cuff her with the back of it. "You've caused enough grief."

"And joy." She laughed. "Surely, joy." She pulled a sheet around her and squeezed past Balthasar.

"Marta, come," the innkeeper's voice called from down the stairs.

"Marta? What a useless name! Marta no more, I think. I wish to be called Rosaline. Such a pretty name! An expensive name. Rosaline will earn me more than Marta." Romeo heard her laughing as she faded down the stairs.

"Juliet, dead?" Romeo searched his emotions. "Why am I not freed? Why do I still feel enraptured with her?" Grief hit him hard. "What have I done?"

"Betrayed true love, perhaps?" Balthasar bit back his anger. Why couldn't his lord be more honourable, less impulsive?

"I must make amends. I must," Romeo stood, fiddling around for his clothes in the pile of bedding. "I must go to her, die at her side. I … Balthasar, I am a fool."

"A banished fool, my lord."

Romeo turned on Balthasar, a spark of his former self showing through. "What is the penalty, except what I seek?"

Balthasar nodded. It was going to be a long ride back to Verona.

As they walked out of the room, Romeo wailed. "Oh, Juliet, I have done you so wrong."

A very long ride, indeed.

Exuent ALL

No Present for Second Place

The would-be invaders arrived too late. The planet had already been conquered. Evidence clearly showed militaries surrendering to one powerful superman. Civilians were taking shelter.

But how could he be so successful? Perhaps his telepathy protected him. He knew so much about so many people! Perhaps it was his speed of movement, so fast even the aliens' orbiting technology couldn't track him.

Another unexpected datapoint: his victims were resilient, surviving his repeated incursions.

The aliens listened, transfixed, as the war below played out for all to hear.

"This is a NORAD special report. Santa Claus has left the North Pole…"

The War on Christmas

"This is WTVU tracking Santa's progress on Christmas Eve." It was a typical seasonal fluff story, the kind that the kids just out of J-school got assigned. Christine shouldn't be doing it. This was punishment, especially for a single mom. She smiled. *I'll take their crap and bake a cake.* "I'm joined by General Gregory Clark from NORAD control here in Colorado Springs. General, what can we expect?"

"General, inbound bogey!" A voice interrupted. "Southerly track, eastern seaboard." Right on time, Christine looked at her watch and smiled. 6:12 p.m., so just after 8pm on the eastern seaboard, almost perfectly timed for the first commercial break during prime time. *The kids were going to love this!* Christine nodded her approval: *This crew was well-prepared.*

"Calmly, folks." The General turned to his men. "We've trained for this. We know what to do. Put it on the big screen. Scramble intercept fighters."

Behind Christine, and perfectly framed in the camera, a map of North America lit up, superimposed with air traffic, moved steadily around it. One blip far up north was highlighted, flashing.

"Fighters away, sir! CAP estimates intercept over northern Labrador in four minutes."

Christine turned back to the camera. "Oh, a bit of excitement. Could this be Saint Nick making an appearance?"

Behind her, but still visible on camera, the General opened a flask and took a quick swig. When he saw the camera watching him, he raised the flask in salutation.

"Tis the season." He winked at the camera and moved off to oversee his men.

"And we're out." Off air, the cameraman was frantically gesticulating towards Christine, asking if she'd seen that. She brushed him off. She hadn't seen it. The corporal sitting at the second radar station was having a hard time not looking at her. She smiled encouragingly at him. He may be fifteen years younger, but that would just mean that he'd hit puberty during the height of her popularity.

Am I on your bucket list? She wondered. Should you be on my naughty list?

"It's a seven-minute break," The cameraman interrupted her reverie, as if his words were supposed to mean something to her. She shrugged her non-comprehension. He made an 'aren't you stupid' face and explained, "They intercept before we're back on air."

Of course, damn it. She felt frustration at how the world conspired against her. Yes, she'd slept with her producer. Yes, he was married. But why was she the only one being punished? She'd only slept with him to gain the weekend anchor desk. Now she was covering Santa Tracker on Christmas Eve!

The message was clear. She'd been too naughty in a profession that still punished women for the crimes of men.

But she'd also heard that the weekend desk might be opening up at rival WFVT. A good night tonight might raise her audience goodwill rating enough to land that gig instead. Screw WTVU.

Three minutes back.

"General, we have visual!" One of the ground controllers shouted. Christine looked at her cameraman, who was talking through his earpiece to the station. He nodded. They were going to go live—a Special Bulletin. Yeah!

A soft count, three, two, one…

"We're back at NORAD, where we've had some fun developments with the Santa Tracker." She picked her moment and tapped the shy corporal on his shoulder. "Can you tell us what's going on?"

He looked startled, from her to the camera, back to her, and then he spoke past her. "Sir! We have confirmed the bogey is real. It's moving at about mach 2. Heat signatures are confirmed."

"Very well. Tell our pilots to do a close pass. I want a visual."

"Yes, sir!"

"Very exciting." Christine grabbed the general's arm and turned him toward the camera. "General, is this how it goes every year?"

"Lady, we don't know what 'this' is yet. Now please keep the camera out of the way." That wasn't according to the script. Christine had watched the last ten years of Santa Tracker coverage. It was always gentle, light-hearted. This felt … tense.

Christine turned back to her camera, deflecting her momentary doubts by tossing her hair. Marketing surveys always said that men loved her hair and women envied it.

"Well, another interesting night!" Time to play up the noble warrior angle. "Our brave sons, brothers, and fathers are working diligently to keep us all safe this Christmas and every night."

The cameraman was giving her the 'wrap' signal. "Now back to A Charlie Brown Christmas already in progress!"

Once they were off air, the cameramen propped his camera against a desk. "This isn't normal," he said. "This is my fifth year, and it's never been this tense."

Christine wasn't sure how to address that.

"And some advice," the cameraman leaned in, "leave the corporal alone. He's having a bad night."

During their downtimes, Christine imagined how she could cut this footage, add it to her highlight reel. In her mind, she was already revising a letter to the News Director at WFVT.

It should almost be time for another check in. She looked at her cameraman, who was looking at her and touching his earpiece, to let her know that the station was talking to him. "We're coming back, regularly scheduled piece in five, four…"

He barely had the camera up when Christine started to speak. "Welcome back. NORAD is busy right now checking out what may very well be Santa. Let's listen in…"

Christine gestured for the camera to come closer and look over her shoulder. That would look so good on her highlight reel. She smiled as she turned, making sure to keep her hair out of the camera frame.

The information was coming fast, and from multiple servicemen:

"Sir, pilots report that the object is about the size of a private jet."

"Sir, the craft has no transponder and has not responded to challenges on commercial channels."

"Sir, the bogey has begun a rapid descent towards Gander!"

Christine turned toward the camera and whispered, "Gander is in Newfoundland, one of Santa's first stops!" She'd done her research. Tonight, she needed to be perfect. She didn't intend to spend next Christmas away from her sons.

"Description, I need a description." The General bellowed, rage-pacing behind the radar operators.

"Sir, it's brown and red. Correction: pilots report that the hull is red with no identifiable markings, no running lights. It appears to be being pulled by a number of brown elk."

"Elk?"

"Yes sir, pilot confirms, elk."

"Damn those Commies! It's a bomb."

Christine spun, barely remembering to wield her microphone, her authority. "Commies? General, surely it's Santa?"

"My pilot identified elk, not reindeer, elk. It's those damned Commies trying to sneak a bomb onto the continent." Christine thought his speech sounded a bit slurred.

"Elk, reindeer," she tried one more time to be reasonable. "Aren't they the same thing?"

"Ma'am," The General looked directly into the camera, his bloodshot eyes dominating the screen, fighting to focus. "My pilots are highly trained at visual identification. If they say elk, then they're elk."

"Your pilots can tell an elk from a reindeer?" The General turned his back on Christine's badgering. He had more important things to do.

With one last swig from the flask, then casting it aside, the General roared, "Weapons go hot. I want that Commie down before he reaches anyone! Engage! Engage! Engage!"

"Engage! Engage! Engage! Aye, sir. Order confirmed."

Christine, her cameraman, and everyone watching A Charlie Brown Christmas on the Fox Network that night saw the blip disappear from the projected radar screen.

"Yes!" The General pumped the air, turning gleefully back towards the camera. "That'll teach that Commie bastard about transponders!"

"You… just… killed… Santa…" Christine pointed to the camera, her anger boiling over, "on live TV!"

She bit back tears, even as her inner voice said, screw the highlight reel. This will make me a star. Fox and Friends, here I come!

"Biggest Commie of them all, if you ask me. Giving free

toys to everyone. Commie, I tell ya." The General's voice trailed out as he leaned on her, his hand reaching down her back for an inappropriate squeeze. "Say, could you introduce me to Sean Hannity?"

Previews

The following passages are excerpts from two properties under development.

They may or may not appear in this form in the final publications.

The following is an excerpt from the novella
A Godless Man

The tempest had mostly passed. Wiper blades swept needlessly against the windscreen, squeaking as they cycled through their task. Jakob Kirkefeld had just dropped his wife and daughter off at the New Rotterdam Aerodrome. Now he sat in the back of this taxi, reliving the memory.

Mixed in among the hugs and kisses had been talk of the storm, unusual so near an aerodrome.

Sloane, Jakob's daughter, was worried about flying. He assured her that air travel was safe, very safe.

The Gods saw to that.

"But don't the Gods control the lightning, too?" Jakob smiled. She's seven now, harder to convince with simple platitudes.

"Yes, honey, and they may be using it all up now so they don't need to later," He had tried to reassure her.

The final reassurance, however, had come from his wife, Sarabeth, "It's OK, dear. The Gods know who your daddy is. They won't hurt us."

Jakob gave Sarabeth a sour look. He hadn't liked that line of reasoning, currying special favour, but it had appeased Sloane, and that was most important.

From the viewing deck, Jakob felt a little motion sick, watching the giant airship gently bobbing headlong in the gusting wind.

When it had come time to board the dirigible, Sloane's excitement overwhelmed her, and she ran ahead, daddy's pending absence forgotten in the rush to find her berth.

"That age." Jakob marvelled as Sloane traversed the swaying gantry with an ease and grace that only the fearless and the young could muster.

"I wish you were coming with us." Sarabeth held Jakob tightly.

He nuzzled her neck. "I know, love. If they hadn't called a Synod for tomorrow…"

One last kiss, and Sarabeth walked carefully onto the gantry, squeezing both handrails, to the great airship beyond, bound for Haida Gwaii, and from there to the Orient, and her symposium in Siam.

Jakob watched as Sarabeth and Sloane approach the purser's desk. One last wave, and they disappeared among the growing crowd.

***

The taxi made good time on the expressway, almost deserted this deep into a Sun Day evening.

They entered Jakob's neighbourhood; tree-lined boulevards with houses set back from the road, each with well-manicured lawns. Jakob saw the occasional jackrabbit nibbling at flowerbeds, liberated by the sprinkling rain that kept the feral cats at bay.

A blast of lightning, directly overhead, interrupted Jakob's revery: Ear-splitting thunder suffocating him, the forceful rumble compressing him, even in the safety of the cab.

Something fell in front of the taxi.

The driver braked hard, both swearing and apologising. Jakob fumbled to undo his seatbelt, flinging his door open before the cab had completely stopped.

"Was that a stag?" Jakob asked desperately, trying to decipher what he'd seen. Stags weren't uncommon, especially in autumn.

Alsun, he prayed, *let it be a stag*.

But it'd fallen from above.

"A person, I think." The cabbie swung the taxi to bring light to bear. In the headlights, the lump did indeed look like a body: someone had fallen from the sky.

Dread filled Jakob. *Sarabeth? Sloane? Alsun carry them!*

The following is an excerpt from the novel
Tau Ceti

"Status?" Michelle called out in her headset even as she tried to focus her eyes on the boards in front of her. No one answered. That wasn't good.

She shook her head, trying for some semblance of rational thought. All she could think was about the pain. She knew, without even giving it waking thought, that her right arm was broken and maybe dislocated.

Thank God for zero gravity, was the first coherent thought that she could later recall. The alarming realisation followed immediately that she shouldn't be in zero gravity. Something was wrong, very wrong.

And with that, Michelle pulled up from a semi-aware state to full consciousness. The alert test pilot, decades of training, taking over. Everything looked wrong, like a worst-case scenario in the trainer, only much worse. Things were broken, floating uselessly.

Her right arm, for one.

Michelle bit back her panic and looked at the forward windows. They were intact, no signs of stress fractures. Obviously, she still had air. She looked for her helmet, and found it floating to her right, above Jeff's limp, sprawled form.

She reached with her left hand for her helmet, her useless right arm, which would shift freely in the zero G, hitting the armrest and sending new shocks of pain down her sides.

She had to get her helmet. Then she could worry about her commander.

Michelle secured her helmet, finally, and looked at Jeff's floating body. It was bad. Not so much the torso or the limbs, although she couldn't really be sure about those. Jeff's body was floating but his head

140

was pinned by the emergency pressure hatch. T

he hatch had automatically triggered when the accident had happened. Its job was to isolate the command cockpit from the bridge in case of emergency. Now, it was trying to close, continually spending energy trying to crush Jeff's head so that it could make the seal that it was designed to form.

"We are in Condition Four. Anyone respond." No one was answering.

That really wasn't good. Michelle looked around, in case the reason was damage to her equipment. She discovered that her headset was unplugged, tangled in herright arm. Damn. A long, painful moment later and Michelle was plugged in.

Immediately, she heard a lot of chatter.

Thomas Blake, life support specialist, was talking to Marc Pinera, their doctor. Apparently, Henri was in a bad way.

"This is Michelle. I'm taking command. Condition Four, Program One. Status?"

"We have air," Thomas replied. Michelle thought that she could hear him hitting something in the background, as if there were pressure gauges that he was thumping to ensure their accuracy. Maybe it was all in her head. "The generators are offline, but the batteries are working. Henri's hurt badly. His face is really messed up, blood everywhere, even in zero G. Marc is with him. Greg is checking on the status of the shuttlecraft. Bill says that the communication array seems to be fried, but he's working on it. Jennifer's with me. No one's heard from Shelley, Sumin, Amanda or Janelle. Or you two. How are you?"

"Marc, I need you up here now."

"In a minute, I'm trying to stop Henri's bleeding."

"How bad is it?"

"I can't tell without more power and light. Gravity would be nice too."

"I think the gravity array's gone," Thomas again, stating the obvious, again. Michelle bit back her temper.

"I need Marc. Now."

"Just a minute."

"Hi, Michelle, this is Jennifer," Jennifer Trent always started with her name, as if her voice wasn't distinct enough. "I've got a functioning board here, but it shows that your hatch didn't close, anyway."

"Nope, it's still trying to close, and it has Jeff pinned. Marc, I really need you up here now. It's got him by the head." Michelle felt as much as heard the various gasps on the open frequency. She could also feel the hysteria rising in her own voice.

Please, Michelle begged any listening diety, *let them just do their jobs. Please, my head hurts too much for any fighting now.*

Marc arrived before Jennifer released the door. He glanced through the opening at Michelle. He had seen Jeff as he approached. It was obvious that they had a major trauma there, but if Michelle needed immediate treatment, it might be wisest for all involved if she was tended to first.

Marc reached through the hatchway, examined Jeff's torso and limbs as best he could. They seemed undamaged, but the body was completely unresponsive to any stimuli.

That wasn't good.

Jeff was still breathing. That counted for something, but … He could see that Jeff's skull was severely damaged. He was afraid to touch it while the hatch was still exerting pressure.

"Zero G doesn't help this," he nagged to no one in particular. "I need his skull to be draining blood, not pooling it. And stop that damned door!"

Michelle could barely keep conscious. Her thoughts were fuzzy, her arm hurt a whole hell of a lot, but that was a good thing. The pain was stopping her from closing her eyes. As she thought about it, she became aware that her head hurt, too. There was an area above her left eyebrow that ached. She tried to touch it and hit her hand on her helmet.

She saw Marc watching her intently.

"I'm not at my best," she said weakly and smiled faintly. He nodded back grimly.

She was vaguely aware of the sound of the hatch behind her opening, and of Marc muttering, "Finally." But she was starting to slip into the darkness again, and that was just fine.

Next Steps

Thank you for reading this collection. If you've enjoyed the stories that you've read, consider joining our mailing list at stephengparks.com.

You'll receive advance notice on short stories, novellas & novels as we publish them.

Reviews on Amazon and GoodReads are always welcome.

Notes on Publication History

Forget Me Nots, How It Really Happened, My First Cosplay, Long Term Storage, Fortunate Waze, and *No Present For Second Place* all first appeared on SpeckLit.com between July 2015 and December 2016. All rights have reverted to the author.

Last Breath Day appears in the anthology *Alien Invasion Short Stories* (Flame Tree Press), published in 2018 in the UK. The story also appeared as episode 64 of Tall Tales TV, produced in 2018 in the US. All rights have either reverted to, or are retained by, the author.

The Wind Wasn't Right first appeared in response to a writing prompt on Janice Hardy's Fiction University blog, 2016. All rights retained by the author.

The Devouring first appeared in Flash-in-a-Flash, December 2020. All rights have reverted to the author.

Shakespeare's Last Stand placed as an honourable mention in a flash fiction contest in 2017. All rights retained by the author.